# RYAN RIDES BACK

# RYAN RIDES BACK

## BACK

BILL CRIDER

M. EVANS
*Lanham • Boulder • New York • Toronto • Plymouth, UK*

Published by M. Evans
An imprint of Rowman & Littlefield
4501 Forbes Boulevard, Suite 200, Lanham, Maryland 20706
www.rowman.com

10 Thornbury Road, Plymouth PL6 7PP, United Kingdom

Distributed by National Book Network

British Library Cataloguing in Publication Information Available

**Library of Congress Cataloging-in-Publication Data**

The hardback edition of this book was previously cataloged by the Library of
Congress as follows:

Crider, Bill, 1941–
 Ryan rides back.
  (An Evans novel of the West)
 I. Title. II. Series.
 PS3553.R497R93    1988   813'.54   88-6955

ISBN: 978-0-87131-542-4 (cloth : alk. paper)
ISBN: 978-1-59077-224-9 (pbk. : alk. paper)

$\infty$™ The paper used in this publication meets the minimum requirements of
American National Standard for Information Sciences—Permanence of
Paper for Printed Library Materials, ANSI/NISO Z39.48-1992.

Printed in the United States of America

*For Judy*

# Chapter One

Three-finger Johnny McGee was sitting on the plank sidewalk in front of Wilson's Cafe the day that Ryan rode back to Tularosa for the hanging. Wilson's was right at the edge of town, the day was clear, and McGee could see Ryan coming for a long time.

Of course, at first he didn't know it was Ryan, and might not have believed it if you told him it was.

It was hot, and McGee was sitting on the walk with his back to the false front of the cafe, trying to find a little shade in the middle of the morning. He sat with his legs spread into a *V* in front of him, throwing a jackknife at the planking, listening to the *thunk, thunk, thunk* that it made as its blade bit into the wood. His boots and part of the legs of his jeans were in the sun, the heat soaking into them, but he didn't seem to mind.

When he happened to look up and see the rider coming, he thought nothing of it. The figures of the man and the horse looked tiny and insignificant, being so far away and so distorted by the heat waves rising off the hard-packed ground. It hadn't rained in Tularosa in a long time.

When the rider got closer, almost to the pile of tin cans that lay rusting outside the town, McGee pushed back his hat and looked out from under the greasy brim trying to get a better look. His hat was worn thin in front from thousands of similar adjustments over the years.

He saw a tall man on a bay mare, but the man's hat shaded his face and McGee didn't expect to recognize him anyway. Besides, a tin can somewhere in the pile caught a beam of the sunlight and shined it straight back at McGee's face, causing him to blink and turn away.

McGee kept right on throwing his knife—*thunk!*—chewing up a good piece of the board in front of him and not caring very much. Enough people would walk on it to wear it smooth again fairly soon.

Then the man rode in front of him and McGee looked up again.

It was Ryan, no doubt about it, even though he was changed. He was wearing a linen duster, and he held his left arm crooked and stiff, with the reins from his horse's bridle held loosely in his left hand. There was a glove on that hand, but not on the right, which swung at his side. His face was still hidden by the hat, but McGee could see part of a jagged scar now, running down the side of Ryan's face out of the shadow of the hat brim.

Ryan held himself tall in the saddle, looking straight down the street, not turning his head an inch to either side, as if he might be looking for something or someone right in front of him.

McGee turned his head slowly, very slowly, like a man reluctant to move at all, as if he were afraid that the least motion might attract unwanted attention to himself. He looked down the street in the direction of Ryan's gaze, but he saw nothing unusual: a woman going into the mercantile store, a man throwing a heavy feed sack in a wagon, a boy throwing a stick for a dog to fetch from the middle of the dusty street, two men entering Colby's Saloon.

Ryan rode right on by, and McGee watched the rider's stiff, straight back for another few seconds before he became aware of a terrible pain in the little finger of his right hand. He had reached over with his left hand to massage the finger before he realized that he didn't have it anymore, that there was nothing there except a stump beginning right below where the second joint had been.

It wasn't the first time the finger had hurt, even though it wasn't there to hurt at all, but it was the first time in a long time. He remembered the day that Ryan had shot the finger off, and how much it had hurt then. He remembered the blood spurting from the stump. Up until then, he'd been just plain Johnny McGee. But after that day he'd had a new name, a new name that would never let him forget Ryan.

The man on the horse looked older than Ryan should look, and he held himself funny, but he was Ryan, all right.

Three-finger Johnny McGee would bet money on that.

The throbbing in his missing finger got worse, and he held his right wrist and wrung his hand. It didn't help. When Ryan was well past him, McGee slipped off the sidewalk, walked between the cafe and the hotel next door, and rode out to tell Kane that Ryan was back.

"It can't be him," Kane said calmly. "Ryan's dead. You know that, McGee."

McGee always felt uncomfortable in Kane's "office," which was really just another room of the huge house. The thick adobe walls made the room quite cool, which was pleasant, but it was dark in there. Kane didn't like the light much. McGee wondered when had been the last time Kane went outside. He thought he knew. His missing finger started to throb again.

"I know he's dead," McGee said. "And I guess you know he's dead, too. But Ryan don't know it. I saw him, plain as I see you, ridin' up the main street."

Kane stood up behind his desk, the only piece of office furniture in the room. He was an impressive sight, no more than five and a half feet tall, but weighing well over two hundred pounds. His face was a pasty white, doughy, with drooping jowls. Dark eyes peered out from two flabby caverns of flesh. Puffy hands hung from the sleeves of the custom-made suit, white fingers writing like thick white grubs turned over with the clods of a spring garden. Thin strands of black hair lay across the white skin on top of his head.

"He's dead," Kane said, his voice rising. "He's dead, god-*dammit!*" The last word thundered out, and McGee backed up a pace. "You saw someone else, someone who might have looked like Ryan. But you *did not* see Ryan!"

McGee swallowed, feeling a dry lump move in his throat. "It was him, all right." He held up his right hand. "Ain't this finger that I ain't even got anymore hurtin' like the blazes? It's him!"

Kane said nothing, simply looked at McGee's hand as if the missing finger might magically appear.

"I guess I know why he's here, too," McGee said, lowering his hand. "I guess I know that, all right."

Kane placed his bloated hands with their palms down on the top of his desk and rested his weight on them. "And why is that?" he said, his voice calm again, almost soothing.

McGee tried to swallow again, but couldn't. "You know," he said. "You know as well as I do."

Kane pushed himself back and eased down into his chair very slowly, as if afraid that he might fall if he weren't careful. "You think he's here for the hanging, do you?" He stared at McGee, who tried to see his eyes in the folds of flesh and then looked away. "I've told you, McGee, there will be no hanging."

"But the judge said—"

"I don't *care* what the judge said!" Kane's voice rose again, and McGee took another step back. "My brother never touched that whore!"

"She wasn't—"

"She was what I say she was, and I don't care what the judge, the town, or anyone else says. And Billy never touched her!"

"Yessir, but the sheriff—"

"I don't care about him, either. He's getting old, and he's a fool. Billy will not *hang* for the death of that whore."

"But they're buildin' the—"

"Let them build," Kane said, his voice very quiet now. "Let

them build. They can hang themselves on it, for all I care."

"But Ryan's here," McGee said, and his own voice had taken on a note of desperation. "Ryan's here now."

"I don't believe that," Kane said. "I believe you saw someone else, someone who looks like Ryan, or someone you might *think* looks like him. Now isn't that right?"

McGee stared at Kane, who sat there in his chair looking like a dimpled albino spider, fat and white, his eyes so hidden in shadow that he might have had only two holes in his face. McGee wanted to agree with Kane, to say that Kane must be right, that sure enough he'd just seen somebody who looked like Ryan since Ryan was dead and certainly couldn't have been riding a bay mare down the main street of Tularosa.

McGee wanted to say that, but he couldn't. He'd seen Ryan, and he knew it. So he didn't say anything at all.

Kane leaned forward slightly in his chair, and McGee could see drops of sweat on his head despite the coolness of the room. "I think you had better check with the sheriff," Kane said. "See if he knows about any strangers in town. Even if the man wasn't Ryan, I don't like the idea of someone I don't know showing up here right now."

"Yessir," McGee said, turning to leave.

"And McGee," Kane said.

McGee turned back. "Yessir?"

"Be here Friday night along with everyone else."

"I'll be here," McGee said, though he didn't like the idea.

"I wouldn't tell anyone else about this man you think you saw, either. Just mention it to the sheriff. That's all."

"I'll do that," McGee said.

"Fine. It might even work to our advantage. It will show the sheriff that our hearts are in the right place, if you know what I mean."

"Yessir."

"Fine. Go do it, then."

McGee left the room as if he were eager to get back to the sun and the heat. Kane watched him go. He was worried, true, but not unduly so. McGee was definitely not the smartest of men, though he did have a certain amount of stubborn courage. There was no doubt that he had seen someone, but it could not have been Ryan.

Ryan had been dead for three years.

He had to be dead, Kane thought. After all, we killed him.


Three-finger Johnny McGee knew better. "We *thought* we killed him," he said, half aloud, as he walked toward the jail, which stood at the opposite end of town from Wilson's Cafe, a good fifty yards from any other building on the street. It was made of sun-dried brick, and Jim Meadows, the deputy, was sitting in front of the door in a rickety wooden chair, a double-barreled shotgun across his lap.

When he saw McGee coming, Meadows angled the shotgun his way. "That's about far enough," he said. "You know Sheriff Bass says none of you Kane men can come to the jail."

McGee stopped. "Look," he said. "I ain't even carryin'. I got to talk to the sheriff."

Meadows peered at him from behind his wire-rimmed spectacles. "Sure enough, no gun. You got that knife in your pocket, though, I bet."

McGee pulled it out. "I'll hand it to you," he said. "I got an urgent message for Sheriff Bass."

"Won't do you no good," Meadows said. "Sheriff won't let you in to see Billy Kane nohow."

"Don't want to see 'im," McGee said. "Just talk to the sheriff."

Meadows thought about it. "Well, all right," he said. "Pitch me that knife first, though."

McGee tossed the knife, and Meadows plucked it out of the air. "You can go on in," he said, "but if I was you I'd knock first. Sheriff don't like surprises."

McGee stepped up on the plank porch and knocked on the door, then opened it and went in without waiting for anyone to ask him.

Sheriff Bass was sitting at his desk, smoking a hand-rolled cigarette and looking through a stack of posters. He glanced up at McGee. "Your picture on any of these?" he said.

"Nosir, not mine," McGee said.

"How come Meadows let you in here, then?" Bass said from behind a swirl of smoke from the tip of his smoke. He was short, only a little taller than Kane, but not nearly as fat. He wasn't wearing his hat, and the beginning of a bald spot showed on the top of his head, though the thick hair on the sides and back of his head showed no signs of thinning.

"I got to tell you something," McGee said.

Bass tossed his cigarette to the floor and crushed it with his boot sole. "Tell me then, but make it quick. And I'm not going to let you see the prisoner."

"I don't want to see 'im," McGee said. "I told Meadows that. It's just that I seen a suspicious stranger in town and thought you ought to know about it."

"What did he do that was suspicious?" Bass said. He didn't like the idea of strangers at this time any more than Kane did.

"It wasn't so much what he did," McGee said. "It was what he looked like."

"Well, then, what did he look like?"

The little finger on McGee's right hand, the finger that wasn't even there, twitched. "He looked a lot like . . . like Ryan."

Bass laughed aloud, slammed his boots on the floor, and stood up. "You think Ryan's come back, do you? After three years? After your boss ran him out of the country like a whipped dog?"

McGee looked down at the dusty floor. He didn't want to say anything, since he knew that Kane hadn't run anybody anywhere. He'd killed him instead.

Bass laughed again, but it wasn't a pleasant sound. "Well, I got to say this: If he's ever comin' back, now's the time. Billy Kane about to be hung for killin'—"

"—a whore. Mr. Kane said she was a whore," McGee said.

Bass came out from behind his desk, stood right in front of

McGee, and looked up at him. "You think he'd say that to Ryan?"

McGee, a head taller than the sheriff, looked down at him. "Maybe not," he said.

"Not on the best day he ever had," Bass said. "Not even then."

"Maybe she wasn't a whore," McGee said. "But she lived in that little shack all by herself. Who's to say what kind of visitors she had and when she had 'em?"

"I'm to say," Bass told him. "I'm the sheriff here, and I'm to say. I knew that girl when she was a baby. I knew her parents when they were alive. I know what kind of a woman she was."

The sheriff walked back over to his chair, sat down, and slowly and deliberately rolled a smoke. He looked in a drawer for a match and struck it on the underside of the desk. He lit his cigarette and inhaled, then blew out a thin stream of smoke.

"She was a fine woman," he said. "She lived alone in that shack because that's all Kane left her when he took the land. And then somebody killed her. Billy Kane. Saturday mornin' we'll hang him." He took another draw on his cigarette. "I'm surprised Ryan has the nerve to show his face back here, runnin' off and leavin' her the way he did, but I guess he heard about the murder. I guess it'd be hard to miss the hangin' of the man who killed your sister."

# Chapter Two

Ryan saw McGee out of the corner of his eye as he passed, and thought: He was one of them. He knew that McGee would run to Kane, which was just fine with Ryan. Somebody had to tell Kane sooner or later.

Ryan kept on riding, straight through town, looking neither to the right nor to the left, his left arm still held in that crooked, stiff way. He rode right past the jail, but Meadows paid him no mind. Meadows hadn't been in town three years ago, and to him Ryan was just another man riding a horse, no one to bother about as long as he didn't try stopping at the jail.

About a quarter of a mile outside of town, Ryan turned off the road at a faint trail and followed it over a rocky stretch where nothing but cactus grew, the thick green stems pushing up out of the hard ground. Then he entered some scrubby oak trees, not very thick and no problem for the horse, hardly tall enough to offer any shade from the burning sun. When he came to the shack, he stopped the horse, threw his right leg over the saddle, and slid awkwardly to the ground. He flipped the reins over the horse's head, and she stood quietly.

He walked over to the shack, looked around, stepped up on the small porch. The door was open, and he went inside. No one had cleaned anything up after the killing of his sister. The cot lay on its side, the blankets on the floor. The wood cookstove sat at an angle, one leg broken off. There were broken plates, but only a few. Sally had put up a fight, he thought.

He straightened up the cot, picked up the broken crockery, and went back outside to see if there was still good water in the well in back. He was thirsty, and he knew the horse was, too.

He had already decided to stay in the shack. He would be safe here, and if they came for him he would be ready. He'd made one mistake the last time, and it had almost killed him.

He didn't plan to let that happen again.


Late in the afternoon they started work on the gallows again. They didn't like to work in the heat of the day, and nobody blamed them. It didn't matter when they worked, anyway, as long as things were ready by Saturday.

Two more days. People were already beginning to drift in from other places. Nobody wanted to miss a hanging.

Billy Kane could hear the hammering and sawing from his cell. It almost made him shiver, in spite of the heat. Billy was a coward.

He had always hated pain, even the littlest ones. He could remember when he was a boy, getting a splinter in his finger up under the nail. He couldn't remember what he'd been doing— building something, putting a roof on the chicken house, something like that. He'd reached for a board and felt the sudden, sharp pain as the splinter rammed up hard under the fingernail. He screamed and tears spurted from his eyes. He didn't want to cry, but he couldn't help it, and trying to stop just made it worse.

He was crying and shaking so hard that he couldn't pull the splinter out, and when he looked he saw the big drops of blood pumping out of the end of his finger. He screamed louder.

Then his brother was there, looking at Billy with contempt. He took Billy's wrist, and while he held it hard and tight he slapped Billy across the face, two stinging slaps, back and forth.

Billy was so surprised that he stopped screaming, and his brother jerked the splinter out of the end of his finger. Billy looked down and saw the thin red line under his nail. He wanted to scream again, but he looked at his brother and he didn't. The tears stopped and began to dry on his face.

"Don't ever let me hear you scream like that again," Kane said. Then he pushed Billy aside and walked away.

Billy wondered if he would have time to scream when they hanged him. He knew how it worked. The trap opened, and you dropped like a rock till you hit the end of the rope, and then . . .

Billy stopped thinking about it. He was getting sick to his stomach.

It was hard not to think, though, with the hammering that was going on outside. Maybe it wouldn't hurt. Maybe it was all so quick that you never felt a thing.

Billy wanted to believe that. He wanted to, but he wasn't sure it was true, which made it worse. If he knew, maybe he wouldn't be so afraid, but he didn't know.

He was going to find out, though.

He almost laughed at that. He was going to find out, and there was no reason why he should.

He hadn't done anything.

He hadn't killed Sally Ryan.


Pat Congrady planned to marry Sally Ryan, and he was the one who found Billy Kane in the shack with her body.

Congrady ran the hardware store. He was a big, beefy man with a red face and red hair. He laughed a lot, and everyone liked him. He'd been planning to marry Sally before her brother left and Kane grabbed their ranch, but that had set his plans back.

It had set Sally back, too. She never understood how Ryan could leave like that, and neither could Congrady. Ryan didn't seem like the man to do something like that, to leave his sister open to a man like Kane, but it had happened. Sally was getting over it, though, slowly but surely, and Congrady was sure that they would be married within the year. She had begun coming into town every afternoon and helping around the store, learning a little bit about the business and taking an interest. Congrady took that as a good sign.

Then one day she hadn't come. Congrady knew the dangers for a woman living alone—a bad fall, a snakebite, a fire. He closed the store and went to see if anything was wrong.

There was something wrong, all right. Sally, dead. The house wrecked, as if there had been a big fight. And Billy Kane right in the middle of it all.

Congrady controlled himself. He didn't kill Billy. He just beat him senseless, threw him across the back of his horse, and took him to town and turned him over to the sheriff.

"I didn't kill her," Billy said. Those were his first words when he woke up in his cell. "I didn't kill her. I just found her like that. I would have come to tell you, but I never got the chance."

"Looks mighty bad for you, Billy," Sheriff Bass told him. "You got blood on you. You were there, right there with that dead girl. And everybody knows you been seein' her on the sly."

Everybody but my brother, Billy thought.

"You ought to have known a Ryan wouldn't have nothin' to do with a Kane, Billy," the sheriff said. "Is that what happened? She tell you what she thought of the Kanes? That girl had a way of sayin' things, I'll say that. She could make a fella mad, all right."

"She didn't say anything," Billy said. "Not this time. She was dead when I got there."

"I hope that's not the best story you got, Billy boy," Sheriff Bass said. "If it is, you're in a heap of trouble."

It was not only the best story Billy had, it was the only story, and he told it over and over. He told it to his brother and to the lawyer his brother hired.

He told it to the judge.

He told it to the jury.

He told it to anybody who'd listen, but it didn't do him any good. The rumors his brother started about Sally Ryan being a whore didn't help, either. Most people in Tularosa liked Sally Ryan. Most of them hated the Kanes. So the rumors didn't help him at all.

"She had to be a whore," Kane told Billy. "How else can you explain why you went there? It couldn't be anything else. She was a Ryan, Billy, and that's as low as you can get. Why else would you want to go to her?"

Billy couldn't explain to his brother, or to anyone else. He didn't have much of a way with words. If he had, he might have talked about the way Sally Ryan's red hair would shine in the sun when she rode to town on the old mule that she had. Or the way her face would light up when she smiled. Or the way she would talk to him like he was almost human, not some kind of idiot, the way his brother talked to him. It wasn't that she liked him, not exactly, but she didn't hold it against him that her brother had run off or that Kane had her land now. It was as if she knew that Billy hadn't had anything to do with that—that his brother was the one who had the insatiable desire to own as much of the land around Tularosa as he could, and that it didn't matter how he got it. The Ryans weren't the first to lose everything to him, and they wouldn't be the last.

Billy had never told her the whole truth about that, though. He was one of the people who knew that Ryan hadn't run away, that Kane hadn't been able to drive him away. Billy had been in the bunch that had killed Ryan one night.

So Billy was as surprised as three-finger Johnny McGee had been when the jailer told him that Ryan was back in town.

"That's what Sheriff Bass says," the jailer, Jack Higby, told Billy. Higby was a young man, not much older than Billy, and he stayed back in the cellblock with him, not so much to keep him company as to make sure there weren't any escape attempts from that direction. He'd gotten to like Billy a little bit and hated to see him in the situation he was in. "Sheriff says somebody saw Ryan ridin' through town not more'n an hour ago. And here we all thought he'd never show his face again in Tularosa. I guess he's come back to see . . ." Higby let his voice die away. He didn't know exactly how to finish his sentence.

Billy knew what Higby had been going to say, though, and he looked out the window high above his head as if he could see the gallows out there. What bothered him, however, was not so much the implication that Ryan had come to see him hang as the fact that Ryan should have been seen in town at all.

"Are you sure it was him?" Billy asked. "Three years . . . that's a long time to be gone."

"I ain't sure," Jack said, "since I didn't see him myself. All I know is, the sheriff says somebody saw him in town."

For some reason Billy felt cold all over.

Virginia Burley, when she heard, felt warm. A flush started on her breast and spread up her neck and covered her face. The news was the talk of Wilson's Cafe, which she had been the nominal owner and proprietor of for five years, ever since Wilson had had the misfortune to encounter a rattler late one summer afternoon while burning some trash. Wilson had been her brother, and she had moved to Tularosa to join him after her husband had been killed in a bank robbery in San Angelo.

Her husband had been a teller, not a robber, and he had been just a little too brave for his own good. He'd had a pistol under the counter, and when he brought it up to use, one of the robbers shot him in the face. The robbers had run then, and the bank owner had thought of Cam Burley as a hero, but he was still dead.

The rattler had bitten Wilson not two months after Virginia had moved to Tularosa, and she was beginning to think she simply had no luck with men—no luck at all. But the cafe had prospered under her ownership, not the least reason being her appearance, and she found she didn't need the men, anyway.

She was tall, with dark black hair and fair skin. Men took to her immediately, but she always put them off. She wasn't going to risk losing another one.

Then Ryan had come along. He was the most self-contained man she had ever met, filled with a quiet confidence and assurance that nothing seemed to disturb. He didn't eat at the cafe, but she saw him around town, heard things about him.

One day he came in, ate the steak that was served for dinner, asked her a question or two, something inconsequential, and left.

The next day he was back, and the day after. Before long, it was obvious to the town that there was something between them, though it was something unspoken and unacted upon.

It was another month before he asked to see her one evening, to take her for a walk around the town. Then it was a ride in his wagon, and then it was other things.

Kane must have seen a certain weakness in her, she thought. He must have known that she was afraid of losing Ryan the way she had lost her husband and her brother, and he had used that fear.

"This thing between me and Ryan is bad," Kane told her one evening, having dropped by the cafe late, after the last of the customers had left. He never ate there himself; his food was prepared for him in his own kitchen by his own staff, and there must have been plenty of it, from the look of him.

"I want you to know that I like Ryan," Kane went on. "I don't want to see him get hurt. You could help me."

"How?" she said. She didn't trust Kane. No one did.

"Talk to him. Tell him that it would be best for him to accept my offer. In the long run, it would be best for all of us."

"He won't listen," she said. "That land was his father's and he says he'll keep it no matter what."

"My offer is more than fair," Kane said, and he was telling the truth. He was offering far more than the market value, and probably even he couldn't have explained exactly why. It was an obsession with him. He didn't want to own all the land around Tularosa—he just wanted to own all the land that joined his property.

"It's not the money," Virginia told him. "He wants the land himself, for him and his sister. And for any . . . family they might have one day."

"I see," Kane said. He had heard the same thing from Ryan

himself when the two had still been speaking. "Yet I believe that you could persuade him."

"It's possible that I could. But I don't think I want to try."

"He could get hurt," Kane said.

"I don't think so," she said. "I think that he's a man who can take care of himself." She hoped that she was right. She wanted to believe that she was.

"That may be true," Kane said.

Not long after that, Ryan had been ambushed on the trail between his ranch and the town. Two men, both Kane's ranch hands, had been killed. Kane, of course, denied having anything to do with the affair. He regretted that two of his men so little appreciated all that he had done for them that they had been forced to resort to robbery to satisfy their base desires. But of course it was not his fault, and he was sincerely sorry it had happened. He hoped that no one would think he was involved in any way at all.

Everyone did think so, but few said so. They didn't want to be ambushed themselves, not being quite as good with a gun as Ryan, or quite as cool under fire.

Nothing happened for weeks after that. Then Kane showed up at the cafe again.

"I suppose you know that I own this place now," he said, sitting in one of the wooden chairs at an oilcloth-covered table, his ample rear lapping over the edges of the chair's seat.

"No," she said. "I didn't."

"Bought the mortgage from the bank just today," he said, smiling broadly. The fat all over his face was cracked with wrinkles.

"Why?" she said.

"An investment. You're doing a very good business here, and I'm sure you'll be on time with all your payments."

In fact, though business was good, she had been late more than once. The banker had overlooked it, since he knew that she would be in the next day. Or the next.

"I would hate to have to foreclose," Kane said. "But I would do it. I would do it if you were so much as a minute late."

She looked at him silently, hating the fat face, the hooded eyes.

"Of course, there is a way that you could own this cafe, free and clear. No more payments. Ever."

She felt a strong disgust, but she said, "How?"

"It's quite easy. And you would be independent then."

He knew more about her than she had thought. Her fear of losing Ryan, her fear that men would always let her down by dying.

"How?" she said again.

He told her, and they took Ryan the next night. She had never told anyone, and she hadn't seen Ryan for three years.

Now she heard someone saying that Ryan was back.

# Chapter Three

Kane hadn't asked Virginia Burley for much.

"I know you go driving with him," he said. "All you need do is have him drive you by Shatter's Grove tomorrow night. It is tomorrow night, isn't it?"

She didn't bother to answer the question. He obviously knew already that they regularly drove out in the wagon in the cool of the evening. "What happens if we do drive by there?" she said.

"Why, nothing. Except that you will receive the deed to this cafe. Free and clear."

"And all I do is have him drive by the grove."

"That is all."

"What happens to him?"

"He and I will have a friendly chat, and I will persuade him that it is in his best interests to sell his land to me."

"A friendly chat."

"With goodwill all around." Kane's fat white face smiled at her, and the effect was worse than if he had frowned. Much worse.

But she did it, anyway.

Ryan was thinking of that night as he sifted through the ruins of the cabin, trying to set things to rights. There seemed to be hardly anything of his sister's there, as if she had no personal possessions left to her. And probably she hadn't. Kane must have taken those along with everything else.

Ryan didn't blame Sally. There had been nothing she could have done. Without him there, she had no one to stand between her and Kane, no one except Pat Congrady; and while he was strong enough physically, he lacked the kind of courage Ryan had, the kind that kept you standing in the face of impossible odds. Congrady loved Sally, Ryan thought, but not enough to stand up to Kane for her.

He righted a rickety wooden table and chair, sitting in the chair to think. It had all started late that evening as he and Virginia drove past Shatter's Grove. . . .

It was just after sundown and beginning to cool off a little. The sky was gray with the last of the light, no stars showing as yet, and the leaves of the oaks in the grove were stirring with a slight breeze. Ryan couldn't remember what he and Virginia had been discussing, but it was probably nothing of great importance. There was something between them, they could both feel that, but it was not something they talked about.

Ryan was not a man to put his feelings into words, and Virginia, thanks to her bad luck with men, didn't trust words any longer. So mostly they drove and looked at the country and said little. Sooner or later, Ryan thought, the time would come when he would have something to say, and he was fairly certain of how she would respond. But for now, especially considering the troubles he was having with Kane, he didn't want to say it.

He was sure that the problems with Kane would blow over. Kane had squeezed out others, but he had never dealt with someone like Ryan before. Ryan wanted his land as much as Kane did, and he was willing to fight for it, as two of Kane's men had already found out. Ryan didn't lament the killing of them. They would have done the same to him, and he knew that Kane was the kind of man who would try violence again if he thought it would gain him anything.

It wouldn't, though. Ryan was constantly on his guard, and he was sure that Kane would eventually give it up, find someone else to harass, some other land to covet.

Ryan was wrong, but he didn't know it then.

He learned it quickly, however. The only time he ever let his guard down was when he was with Virginia. Their times together seemed like times of peacefulness that nothing could interrupt, and nothing ever had. But that night something did.

The riders came out from behind the trees of the grove, their pistols cocked and aimed. They had handkerchiefs pulled up over their faces, but Ryan knew who they were, all right.

Billy Kane, so nervous he might shoot himself in the foot at any moment.

Johnny McGee, nervous, too, but a man with just enough gumption to be troublesome.

Mack Barson, who was big as a bear and smelled like one. It was rumored that he bathed only by accident, like the time when his horse was crossing Saragosa Creek and stepped off in a hole. That had been three or four years back. No one was sure just how long. Some of the Tularosa wits thought Barson's smell was what made him so mean. He didn't even need a pistol to kill a man. His hands were enough.

Martin Long, thin as a rattler, and with a rattler's evil eyes, but meaner than any snake that ever lived. The story was that he liked to hurt people, and no whore in Tularosa would let him come near her.

And Kane, of course. There was no disguising Kane, that mountain of flesh who sat on a horse like three hundred pounds of mud.

"Get down from the wagon, Ryan," Kane said, his voice muffled by the handkerchief, but Kane's voice nevertheless. "Get down quietly, and we let the woman ride away."

Ryan handed the reins to Virginia, climbed down, and faced

them. He didn't think they'd shoot him in front of her, and he didn't think they would shoot a woman. Not even Kane would do something like that. He'd bring every man in the Southwest down on him if he did.

"Turn the wagon back to town," Kane said.

Ryan heard the creaking of the harness, the clopping of the horses' hooves. He didn't look back.

As the sound of the wagon wheels receded in the distance, the men on horseback looked at Ryan. Darkness gathered around them.

Ryan thought that the darkness was his only chance. If he could get to the trees . . .

He let his eyes slide to the shadows under the oaks. The grove wasn't big, but it was big enough, and it was dark in there under the trees.

As soon as he could hear the wagon no longer, Ryan broke to his right, toward the nearest tree.

Pistol shots rang out at his back. A bullet grazed his left arm, and another clipped off the heel of his left boot. He fell sprawling, and rolled toward the tree, coming up in a crouch beside it with his pistol in his right hand.

He fired blindly in the direction of the first figure he could see in the heavy dusk and heard Johnny McGee screaming. "My hand! He's shot off my goddamn hand!" Then there was a thud, which sounded as if someone, probably McGee, had fallen off his horse.

Ryan didn't think it was possible to shoot off a man's hand, but if it was, he hoped that he had taken at least one of the five out of the fight.

He snapped off two more shots, with less spectacular results, and then began to work his way back into the trees.

Twenty feet back into the darkness, he paused to listen. He could hear a horse snorting, and he could hear the moaning of the man on the ground.

That was all he could hear, except for the humming of some kind of insect next to his ear. He brushed at it and moved back as quietly as he could. If he could hold out for thirty minutes, Virginia would be sending the sheriff back. He was sure of that.

Then he heard the clink of a horseshoe against a stone and turned to his left. All he saw was a spurt of flame as the pistol fired at him. When the bullet hit him, he was thrown backward as if he had been kicked by a mule. There was a terrible numbness in his left arm from the elbow down, and in fact he thought that it might have been shot off, just like McGee's hand. He reached over and touched it. It was there, with blood soaking through the shirt.

The pain would come later.

He had landed behind a tree, and he looked around it, hoping to get a shot at whoever had hit him. He saw no one. He moved backward again. He had to hold out. Keep them off until the sheriff came.

He might have made it if it hadn't been for Long. Somehow Long found him without making a sound, and stood behind him in the trees, waiting for him. The first Ryan knew of Long's presence was the barrel of the pistol that stuck him in the back, hard, like an iron rod.

"Hold it right there, or I'll shoot you where you stand," Long said. His voice hissed on the *S*'s, like a snake.

Long had gotten too close, so Ryan whirled around, knocking the pistol away with his right arm as he turned, but Long recovered quickly. Almost as if his snaky eyes could see in the dusky dark, he reached out and grabbed Ryan's left arm.

It was probably just Long's good luck, and Ryan's bad fortune, but Long had done just about the only thing that could completely immobilize Ryan. Just at that moment, the numbness wore off and the pain came flooding up from the elbow, engulfing Ryan completely. His pistol fell from his fingers, and he almost fell himself.

Ryan managed to strike at Long feebly and ineffectually. Long hung on to the arm, dragging Ryan backward.

"I got 'im," Long called out. "Back here!"

"Where?" It was Kane's voice. "Where are you?"

"Back in the trees," Long said.

A dark form stepped out from behind another of the trees. "Here they are," Mack Barson said.

"Get him out here," Kane said. "Surely the two of you can handle him."

"Now we can," Long said. "He's hurt."

Long located his pistol after turning Ryan over to Barson, who twisted the arm in his cruel grip, sending ripples of pain with every twist.

"Let's go," Long said, when he had found the gun.

Ryan stumbled along in front of them, wondering how long it had been, wondering if Virginia had been able to get back to town yet, wondering if she had sent the sheriff on his way.

Out from the shelter of the trees, Ryan could see the night sky filled with stars. The moon had come up, round and yellow. Kane was still sitting on his horse. Billy was standing by Johnny McGee, looking at his hand.

"It's just the finger that's gone," Billy said. "The little one. He's just got three fingers now."

"Well, Mr. Ryan," Kane said. "You've severely damaged one of my men. But it appears as if you might be slightly indisposed yourself."

Ryan said nothing. He had nothing to say to Kane. Nothing at all.

"I had hoped we might talk like civilized men," Kane said. "Simply talk. That was all. But no. You had to run. You had to resort to violence, in the way a man like you always does. Now it appears as if you do not wish to talk at all. That really is too bad."

Ryan looked at the doughy face, pale white in the moonlight. It looked as if it were floating there above Kane's dark clothing like the moon floated in the sky.

"Yes," Kane said. "I had hoped that we could conclude a deal tonight, a deal for your land. I just happen to have a contract here with me." He reached inside his coat and drew out a piece of paper. "I thought that you might sign this, but I doubt very much that you would, not now."

"I never would have, anyway," Ryan said.

"Perhaps a little persuasion," Kane said. "Mack."

Ryan never even saw the fist coming, but he felt it when it collided with his temple. The shock spun him around and for a few seconds even drove the pain of his arm out of his mind.

Long caught his arm, just to remind him, and smashed him in the other temple.

Ryan was reeling, hardly able to stand, but somehow he kept his feet. He wasn't going to let them get him down. He would never go down for them.

And then he did. Because Barson hit him across the chest with a board or a limb, or maybe just his forearm. Whatever it was, it was hard, harder than Ryan, and he felt his ribs crack as he stumbled backward.

He hit the ground, hard, and then his head went back and struck the packed earth. For a second, everything stopped.

Then it all came back, doubled, as he awoke to the toes of Long's boots kicking him in the side.

Then Barson.

Then Long.

And then Kane's voice. "Pick him up."

He felt himself being lifted by hands under his armpits. There was no specific pain now, nothing localized. His entire body was throbbing with hurt.

"We could avoid all this if you would merely sign this paper," Kane said.

Ryan tried to focus his eyes on Kane, but he couldn't. He wondered if he had been kicked in the head, too, or if his inability to focus was merely the effect of his head hitting the ground. It didn't really seem to matter.

He tried to say he'd be damned if he'd sign, but no words came. So he shook his head.

"I see," Kane said. "Your turn, Billy."

Ryan tried to look where Billy had been standing by McGee.

"I . . . I don't know," Billy said.

"Don't know what?" Kane said.

"I mean, haven't we done enough? He looks nearly dead to me."

"He's not dead, Billy," Kane said. "Not yet, anyway. See if you can change his mind."

"I . . . can't," Billy said.

"Yes, you can." Kane's voice was patient. "One way or another, you can do it."

"No," Billy said.

"Yes," Kane said. "Use your pistol if you're afraid to use your hands."

Barson and Long moved away from Ryan, their eyes filled with contempt for Billy, a contempt that in the darkness he could not see. Only feel. He took his pistol out of its holster.

"Don't kill him," Kane said. "We don't want him dead. Yet."

Billy looked at Ryan. The night was quiet again, as quiet as the stars, as if even the horses were holding their breath.

"No," Billy said.

Kane jerked his own pistol out and fired it. Ryan saw the spurt of flame and felt his left arm flung backward. He felt the impact of the bullet, but had no idea where it had hit. There was too much other pain for him to tell.

"Like that, Billy," Kane said. "It's really very easy."

Billy cocked his pistol. He fired, and dirt kicked up by Ryan's left boot.

"Close, Billy," Kane said. "But not good enough."

Kane would have fired again himself, but suddenly Ryan was moving, shambling forward in an awkward attempt at a run. He had seen Billy's horse move right behind Billy, not fifteen feet from where they were standing.

Ryan knew there was no way he could get on the horse, but he hoped there was something he could do. He wasn't going to stand there and get killed. If they were going to kill him, they were going to kill him while he was on the move.

Before anyone could figure out what he was doing, he had gotten to the horse's left side. Then the bullets started flying, one of them chipping a stone right by the horse's rear hooves.

The horse jumped, started forward.

Ryan jumped, too, managing to hook his right arm through the stirrup.

The chipping stone, the sudden unexpected weight, the gun-shots coming all around it—all of these things were too much for the horse, which panicked and ran, dragging Ryan along beside it, bouncing him across the rocky ground like a rag doll.

Kane was no good in a chase. He was too heavy, and his horse was made for carrying weight, not for racing. Barson and Long took too long getting mounted. Billy had no horse. McGee was still nursing his hand.

Before they could get organized, Ryan was out of sight in the darkness. And though they searched for hours, they never found him.

They spent the next two days in a kind of eager fear, Barson and Long constantly watching their backs; Billy keeping to his room, sweating, with a chair propped under the door handle and a blanket tied up over the window; McGee complaining about his hand and saying that he'd never be able to use a pistol again; Kane waiting for the sheriff to arrive.

The sheriff never arrived, but Billy's horse did, looking drawn and thirsty, with the saddle twisted completely around and hanging under its belly.

Kane was convinced, as were the others, that Ryan must be dead, that some of the shots had hit him and that he was now lying somewhere in the great unpopulated expanse of West Texas, food for buzzards or whatever else could get at him.

It was shortly after that time that Kane started the rumor of Ryan's running away, saying that he must not have been able to stand up to the fear he had of Kane. And shortly after that, Kane managed to get his hands on Ryan's land, leaving Sally only the shack for a place to live.

Virginia Burley never told her part in the events of that night, and when she heard the story of Ryan's running she shook her head and felt a secret hurt in her heart. She didn't know what had happened, but she knew she had been a part of it. She also knew that it wasn't like Ryan simply to leave, no matter what people were saying. She thought that Kane might very well have killed him, but she could never say so. All she could do was count herself lucky that she owned her cafe, free and clear, and would never have to depend on any man again. There were plenty around who would have liked to make her offers, but she ignored them one and all.

Ryan set some canned tomatoes on a shelf in the shack. He had no idea how Virginia felt, but he did know one thing. She'd never sent the sheriff back to the grove that night. It was more than a feeling now; had she done so, surely Bass would have mentioned it to him.

He wondered if that mattered now, after all that had happened. He wondered if he would see her again. The cafe was there; McGee had been sitting in front of it, and he wondered if McGee's being there had any significance.

Probably not, he thought, but you never knew about those things. Maybe he would find out. Maybe not.

He wondered if he cared.

# Chapter Four

It had been a fairly boring day for Deputy Jim Meadows, except for McGee showing up. Everybody else had pretty much avoided the jail, as if the prisoner might have something catching, something that might infect them if they got too close. Meadows thought that was funny. Anybody could see that Billy Kane was scared half to death and the only thing you could catch from him was a yellow streak.

Despite the lack of excitement, in fact the lack of any activity at all, Meadows had to sit in front of the jail with the shotgun ready to deal with anything out of the ordinary. Sheriff Bass was almost certain that something would eventually be done by Kane and his men to break out Billy. Kane was a stubborn man, and he didn't want his baby brother to die.

It was a funny thing, Meadows thought. He had been to the trial and had even gotten to know Billy Kane a little bit. It was hard for him to think of Billy as the kind to be a killer. Of course he was supposed to have killed a woman, and if Billy was going to kill anybody, Meadows supposed it would be a woman—somebody who couldn't put up much of a fight if attacked. Trouble with that idea was, it looked like Sally Ryan had put up a hell of a fight. Meadows had been in the shack with the sheriff, and the place looked like a brawl had been fought there.

Billy didn't strike Meadows as a brawler, and Congrady had brought him in alone. Billy had been pretty marked up, all right, but Meadows figured Congrady had done most of that.

Well, it wasn't any of his business. His job was to sit out here with his shotgun and watch for trouble, not to question the verdict of a jury, and a jury of good citizens who paid his salary, at that.

He wasn't really watching much when Ryan came riding up. He was about half asleep, to tell the truth; the afternoon sun warming the air and the lunch that had been brought from Wilson's Cafe had combined to make his eyelids heavy. Had Ryan kept on riding, he might have passed by unseen for a second time that day.

This time, however, Ryan stopped right in front of Meadows, who jerked his head up, grabbed his shotgun securely with his right hand, and adjusted his glasses with his left.

He looked up and saw a tall man sitting on a bay horse. The man was holding one arm funny, and he had a glove on one hand. He sat kind of stiff, too, as if there was something holding his back straight.

"Who the hell are you?" Meadows said.

The man shifted the tiniest bit in the saddle, and the horse twitched its tail. "Name's Ryan," the man said.

"Ryan," Meadows repeated. He looked at the man again, saw two pale blue eyes, so pale they were almost white, looking back at him. "Any kin to . . . uh . . ."

"I'm her brother," Ryan said.

"Little late for a homecomin', ain't it?" Meadows said. He wasn't normally belligerent, but he was trying to make up for having been caught dozing.

His comment seemed to have no effect on Ryan, who said nothing.

"What you want from me?" Meadows said.

"I want to talk to the sheriff," Ryan said.

"I don't know about that. Sheriff don't want just anybody goin' in there right now, not with the prisoner he's got. And since the prisoner's convicted of killin' your sister . . ."

Ryan got awkwardly off his horse and flipped the reins around the cedar hitching rail. "I think the sheriff would let me in," he said.

Meadows noted the low-slung pistol on Ryan's right hip. "Maybe," he said. "You'll have to leave the gun out here, though."

Ryan unbuckled the gun belt with his right hand, holding the left arm immobile across his body. He handed the belt and the holstered pistol to Meadows, who took it and set it down beside him.

"Something wrong with your arm?" Meadows said.

"Yes," Ryan said. "Something."

Fine with me if he don't want to talk, Meadows thought. I guess it won't hurt if a fella who's halfway a cripple goes in the jail. Don't see how he could do much damage, even if he was of a mind to. "Go ahead on in," he said. "Sheriff's right inside."

Bass looked up when Ryan came through the door. "Hello, Ryan," he said. "I heard you were in town."

"News still travels fast here," Ryan said.

"I guess I was almost expecting you," Bass said. "Course, lots of folks around here didn't figure ever to see you again."

"Why's that?" Ryan said.

Bass laced his fingers together, put his hands behind his head, and leaned back in his chair. "I guess they figured that once you left, you were gone for good."

"I guess they were wrong," Ryan said.

"Looks that way, don't it?"

Ryan didn't answer, and for a minute the two men watched one another warily, like two dogs sizing one another up on the street.

Bass took out his tobacco pouch and papers, rolled a cigarette, lit it, breathed smoke. He noted the left arm, remembered the stiff way Ryan had walked into the room. "Looks like you had a little trouble, wherever you were."

"A little," Ryan said. He intended to deal with his trouble his own way. It was too late to tell the sheriff about it now.

"I hope you haven't come back to make any trouble for us here in Tularosa," Bass said. He tossed his tobacco pouch idly in the air, catching it in his left hand.

"I just came by to find out what you knew about my sister's murder," Ryan said. "How much trouble is that?"

"Not much," Bass said. "Why don't you have a seat?"

There was a wooden chair with a rounded back near the desk. Ryan walked over and eased himself down.

"I guess you know we got the killer in jail here," Bass said.

"Billy Kane," Ryan said. "I heard that."

"I know you and Kane had your troubles," Bass said. "I hope you don't think you're going to hurry justice along any."

"No," Ryan said.

"That's good. The hangin's set for day after tomorrow, and that ought to be soon enough for anybody."

"I'd like to know why."

"Why?" Bass was confused. "Because Saturday's the day we have hangin's around here. Got to give folks a chance to get to town. Nobody wants to miss a good hangin'."

"That's not what I mean. I mean I'd like to know why he did it."

Bass looked at the twisted end of his cigarette as if he might find the answer there. Then he took a last puff and tossed the butt to the floor, stepping on it with his boot sole. "I can't tell you that," he said.

"Why not?"

"Because I don't know. I know what I think, that's all. Billy never admitted doing it."

"Wait a minute," Ryan said. "He's going to hang for murder, but he didn't confess?"

"That's right," Bass said. "Pat Congrady caught him right there with the body, and brought him in. That was good enough for the jury."

"Sounds like a pretty weak case to me," Ryan said.

"There's a little bit more to it than that. Everybody around here knew that Billy Kane was after your sister to marry him, and everybody knew she never would. Not after what happened." Bass paused and looked at Ryan. "I might as well tell you that folks don't think too much of you in these parts, goin' off and leavin' her like that, lettin' Kane get hold of that land."

"I don't blame them," Ryan said.

Bass didn't know what to make of that remark, so he went on with his story. "Well, Billy swore up and down that he didn't kill your sister, that she was dead when he walked in the shack. But he admitted that he'd been there awhile, sort of shocked by her murder, he said. I guess you could say it just came down to what folks wanted to believe, and they wanted to believe that he was guilty. Most of them've been looking for a way to get back at the Kane family for years, and this was their chance."

"Do you think he did it?" Ryan said.

"I did at first," Bass said. "Now? Now I'm not so sure."

"Why not?"

"Well, I've dealt with a few hardcases in my time—not many, but a few. And it seems to me that every single time, when the chips were down, they told the truth. That guff you hear about a man goin' right up on the gallows sayin' he's an innocent man all the way? Don't you believe it. They always confess in the end, either to me or the jailer or the preacher. They want to tell somebody, seems like.

"But Billy? Not him. And let me tell you somethin'. Billy's not any hardcase. He's soft inside as anybody I ever saw. He's so scared right now, he can't hardly eat or sleep. I've talked to him, told him how he'd feel better if he got it off his chest, but it didn't work. He still swears he didn't do it."

"And there was no evidence against him?"

"There was some evidence, I guess you could call it."

"I'd think it would take more than guessing, in a murder," Ryan said.

"Whoever killed your sister, well, he did it hard," Bass said, looking at Ryan to see how he'd take it.

Ryan just sat there, looking at Bass with those pale eyes.

Bass made himself another smoke. "Whoever did it had to be marked up some, and Billy was marked up, all right."

"So that was the evidence?"

"That was it." Bass blew smoke.

"So what was wrong with it?"

"Who says anything's wrong with it?"

"You do. You said it was evidence, 'I guess you could call it.'"

"Did I say that?"

Ryan moved in his chair. Something changed in his eyes.

"All right, I said it."

"So what was wrong."

"When Congrady brought him in, he wasn't in any condition to have killed anybody. Congrady had pretty well beat him up. He could've got the marks from Congrady, that's all."

"Did Congrady say how he looked at first? Before he beat him up?"

"Says his face was all red, like he'd been hit before."

"And that was good enough for a jury?"

"The jury we had? Yeah, it was good enough."

"It's not like Kane to take this so easy," Ryan said. "I know he doesn't think much of Billy, but I'm surprised he's going to let him hang. I thought he had more control of the town than that."

"So did he," Bass said. A smile crossed his face. "I think he was the most surprised man in town when that guilty verdict came in. But there was a judge he couldn't buy, and a jury that hated the name of Kane. I swear, I thought he would have a stroke right there in the courtroom. That fat face got so red it looked like he was on fire."

"But he's let Billy sit right here in jail, right up to the time for the hanging."

"That's right. Don't think I wasn't worried. But I got my deputy out there watchin', and I'm right here myself all day and night. And the jailer stays, too. Two of us sleep back in the cells, and one of us watches here in the office."

"Your deputy must have had the last watch," Ryan said, thinking of Meadows's heavy eyes.

"That's right," Bass said. "How'd you know?"

"Lucky guess. Think I could talk to the prisoner?"

"I don't know about that, Ryan. That could be a dangerous proposition."

"I'm not armed. You've got the jailer back there. You're here. You've got your deputy right outside the front door. You think I could get past the three of you?"

Bass looked at him appraisingly. "There was a time . . ." he said.

Ryan didn't seem to hear him. "Can I see Billy Kane?"

Bass stood up. "I guess it wouldn't hurt. But just for five minutes now. No more."

"That should be enough," Ryan said. He stood up.

Bass got a heavy iron key from his desk drawer, and he and Ryan walked over to the thick wooden door in the wall that separated the cells from the office. There was a small window in the door, with four short iron bars in it.

"I'm comin' in with a visitor, Jack," Bass called through the window.

"All right, sheriff, come ahead," Higby called back.

Bass put the key in the lock and turned it, then swung the door open. The hinges needed oil; they squeaked as the door moved inward.

Bass and Ryan stepped through the door. There were only four cells, all of them small, holding nothing more than a cot and a slop bucket. Jack Higby sat at the far end of the hall in a wooden chair like the one Meadows occupied out front. He held a shotgun like the one Meadows had, too.

"Jack's gonna have to stay here with you," Bass said. "I'm goin' back to the office. Knock on the door when your five minutes is up."

"I'll do that," Ryan said.

Bass went through the door and swung it shut behind him.

Ryan looked at Higby, whom he had met a time or two years before. "Hello, Jack," he said.

Higby didn't recognize him at first. He leaned forward in the chair, still keeping a careful grip on the shotgun. "Ryan?"

"That's right. Sheriff Bass said I could talk to Billy."

"All right with me," Higby said. He was glad for the interruption. It was hot in the jail, and about the only entertainment he got was taking out his bandanna every few minutes and wiping off the sweat that was running down his face. One thing for sure, Billy Kane wasn't any fun. Mostly he just sat on his cot and felt sorry for himself. Higby had tried to talk to him at first, Higby being a man who liked to talk, but Billy hardly ever bothered to answer. And when he did he just said something like "I swear to God I didn't do it, Jack."

It got real tiresome after a while, so Higby was glad to see another face and maybe have the chance to talk a little bit. Or at least listen to Ryan talk.

"You can't go in the cell," Higby said, "but you can talk to him all right from here."

Ryan looked through the bars at Billy Kane, who sat cowering on the cot, looking back at him.

"How are you, Billy?" Ryan said.

Billy seemed to shrink into himself, pushing his back against the wall as if he wanted to push right through it and be outside. He didn't answer Ryan.

Ryan let the silence grow for a full minute. Then there was a barking laugh from Higby.

"He won't talk to you," Higby said. "I been after him for days, but he won't say a blessed word."

There was a small barred window in the cell, and the light slanting through it made a barred pattern on the floor. Billy sat in shadow, but Ryan could see that he had recovered from the worst of his beating. He tried again.

"They say you claim to be innocent," he said.

Billy moved a little on the cot and brought his eyes up to look back at Ryan, but he remained silent.

"Told you he wouldn't talk," Higby said. "I bet he ain't said a word to me in two days. Just sits in there and listens to the hammerin' outside. They oughta be about finished with that thing by now."

Ryan thought again of that night at Shatter's Grove, of how Billy had fired at him and missed, of how Kane had pushed him to shoot. He wondered for the first time if Billy had missed deliberately.

"She was my sister," Ryan said. "I'd like to know how it happened. You're the only one that can tell me."

Billy opened his mouth and seemed to want to speak, but the words didn't come.

"Give it up, Ryan." Higby leaned his chair against the wall and balanced it on the two back legs. He pulled out his handkerchief and mopped his face. "He won't talk, I tell you."

"I guess you're right." Ryan turned to go.

"Wait," Billy said.

Ryan heard Higby's chair legs hit the floor.

"I'll be damned," Higby said. "He *can* talk, after all."

Ryan turned back.

Billy Kane got off the cot and walked to the bars of the cell, wrapping his hands around them. "I want to tell you," he said. "I know you won't believe me any more than the others did." He stopped and shook his head. "I don't even blame you. I never killed Sally. I never killed anybody."

To Ryan, Billy looked about fifteen years old. He was nowhere as fat as his brother, but he had a smooth, babyish face even though he probably hadn't shaved for days. His skin was pale and white from the time he'd spent in the jail. He didn't look like he could kill a sick dog, much less a healthy woman.

"When I got there, she was dead. That's the truth. I just want you to know. I never wanted to kill her. I wanted to marry her."

"What?" Ryan couldn't believe he'd heard right.

Higby laughed at Ryan's surprise and grabbed his chance to get in on the conversation. "Hell, Ryan, ever'body knew that. Young Billy's been sneakin' over to that shack of your sister's for a year or more."

Ryan stepped closer to the bars. He stared into Billy's eyes as if hoping to see the truth hidden there.

"I didn't kill her," Billy said. There was a hopelessness in his voice that indicated he didn't expect to be believed. He released his grip on the bars and walked back to the cot, where he sat listlessly, not looking at Ryan. Not looking at anything.

The door at the end of the hall opened.

"I expect you've been in here long enough, Ryan," Bass said. "Don't want you to tire out the prisoner."

Ryan didn't move. He stood looking intently into the cell, but Billy didn't raise his head or say anything else.

"Let's go, Ryan," Bass said.

Ryan turned away from the cell and walked to the door. As Bass swung it shut, Ryan said, "Has he said anything about being in love with Sally before this?"

Bass didn't meet his eyes. "He said it at the trial. It was something people in town talked about."

"And they still think he killed her?"

"She hated him, Ryan. You think she'd have anything to do with one of the Kanes? He probably killed her because she wouldn't."

"You believe that?"

Bass shook his head. "I don't know. It's possible, ain't it?"

"Maybe," Ryan said. "Thanks for letting me see him."

"Sure," Bass said.

Ryan went outside and got his gun belt. He put it on awkwardly, holding it in place with his still left arm.

Bass came out the door and stood beside Meadows, both of them watching Ryan. Neither man would have dreamed of offering to help.

Ryan got the belt buckled and climbed on his horse, another awkward process, since he had to mount from the right side. The horse didn't seem to mind.

As he was about to ride away, Bass said, "You've been gone a long time, Ryan. Things have changed. Maybe even your sister changed, but not enough to love a Kane. You should have come back sooner."

Ryan turned the horse's head and rode out of town.

# Chapter Five

Ryan hadn't been able to come back. Not for a long time, anyway.

He had opened his eyes slowly against the bright light of the sun. He had no idea where he was, or how he had gotten there. All he knew was that his body was a single throbbing ache.

The sun stabbed at his eyes. There was someone—something—sitting nearby, watching him.

Ryan's eyes were gritty, but he found that he couldn't move his arm to wipe them. He tried, and the ache expanded inside him. It was as if a hot iron were being driven up the length of his arm.

He blinked. Even that took an effort. Even that hurt.

He thought he could make out a man, crouched, sitting on his heels, his chin almost resting on his knees. He was only a few yards away, watching.

Ryan tried to say something.

Nothing emerged from his mouth but a rasping wheeze.

He wondered if he was dead, but he knew immediately that he

couldn't be. Dead people couldn't hurt the way he did. He closed his eyes.

He thought he could feel the sun burning his face, but he wasn't sure. Maybe it was just the pain, the pain that now seemed to be rippling through him in waves.

He opened his eyes again.

The man was still there, dressed all in black, his head leaned forward over his knees, watching.

Ryan tried to raise his head. He couldn't do that, either.

As he closed his eyes, he felt consciousness slipping away. And he thought, It's not a man. It's a buzzard.

The next time Ryan woke up, it was dark. There was no sun to torment his eyes, but at the same time he still couldn't see.

His mind had cleared. He could remember the events at Shatter's Grove, and he knew how he had gotten to wherever it was that he was now lying. The horse had dragged him for a long way, ripping his clothing to shreds. He remembered the rocks ripping at his skin, the cactus spines stinging him, the hard ground grinding against his legs.

It got worse when the saddle slipped. He was twisted over on his back, and there had been a collision with a big rock that had caused him to black out. How he had avoided the horse's hooves he had no idea.

When the horse had finally stopped running, he had slipped his arm out of the stirrup, a job that he almost hadn't been able to do. It almost required more strength than he had left and more maneuverability. There were parts of his body he couldn't move at all.

He knew that he was still alive, because he still hurt. Aside from that, nothing else seemed to matter very much.

The *curandero* squatted on his haunches and looked at the man lying beside the cactus. He had thought for a long time that the man was dead, but he watched to make sure. Some men were stronger than others. Some men were hard to kill.

When the man opened his eyes at about the middle of the day, the *curandero* knew that he was alive and that it would be all right to touch him. His spirit was still trapped within him.

It was hard to believe, because the man looked dead. His clothing hung on him in rags, and his skin was lacerated everywhere. His left arm was twisted at an impossible angle, and his skin had been burned by the sun.

The *curandero* had a little water in a leather skin, and he moistened a piece of rag and ran it over the man's lips. The man did not stir, so the *curandero* squeezed a few drops of the water into his mouth. There was nothing more he could do.

He was a very old man, and he hadn't set out to help anyone. He had set out to die.

He did not know how old he was, and it had never seemed to matter before. He knew that there was no man or woman in the tribe whose birth he did not remember, so he was older by far than any of them, and that was all. He had possessed the power of healing, and he had been a help to all of them at one time or another. He knew which plants could be boiled to produce medicines, which could be eaten, and which would kill. He knew which animals made men strong, and which made them weak. He could ease a woman in her birthing, and he could cure stings and sores with the proper poultices.

But he had gotten old. He was virtually toothless, and his legs were bad. He could no longer run, and he could hardly even walk, unless he went very slowly. He found that his mind wandered more and more, that he could recall the days of his youth quite clearly and the days that he lived in hardly at all. To eat was no longer a pleasure, and to sleep was almost impossible. He was no longer of value to the tribe. He was only a burden.

One night he had simply left, walking slowly, very slowly, the only way he could walk, toward the north. During the days, he rested. At night, he walked.

Sometimes, if he was lucky, he slept.

He waited to die, but he did not, and something happened after he crossed the big river. He saw an eagle.

It was early in the morning, before he stopped for the day, and his spirit soared with the bird. The eagle had always been for him a source of power.

From that day, the old man grew stronger. He began to think more about life than death, to trap small animals for food—rabbits mostly, and he caught a lizard now and then.

He began to wonder why he had not died. He knew there was a reason, and he knew he would discover it. He kept walking very slowly to the north, but even his legs seemed to gain strength from the sight of the eagle.

Then he came upon the man.

It was early, the same hour at which he had seen the eagle, and the old man wondered if that was significant. He thought that it might be, and he squatted down to watch the man, to see if he was alive or dead. It took a long time to find out, but the old man was patient. He was going nowhere in particular, except to death, and that seemed to be even farther from him now than when he had begun. He had time.

So when the man stirred and opened his eyes, the *curandero* gave him water, and then later he gave him more. Not much, but maybe enough to keep the man alive.

There is something I can do here, the old man thought. I am a *curandero;* I can help this white man. But looking at the man, the *curandero* began to lose heart. He had helped many men, and he even knew a little about broken bones, but he had never seen a man in such a condition as this before.

He had seen a man once, a man who had somehow broken his leg and fallen down the side of a mountain, starting a small avalanche in the process and falling among a slide of rocks and boulders. That man had looked almost as bad as the one in front of him now.

That man had died.

But there was no way to tell about what was inside a man by looking, no way to judge his spirit while he lay broken before you. This man might not die. This man might share something of the spirit of the eagle. The *curandero* would have to wait and see.

The next day Ryan opened his eyes in shadow.

He had not been moved, and his body was still racked with tremendous pain, but he was in shadow. He couldn't move his head to find out why. He looked, and a few yards away an old man crouched, an old man dressed in ragged black pants and shirt, with a black headband tying back long gray hair.

The old man was clearly watching him, but he no longer looked like a buzzard. He was just an old man now, so old that he seemed to have dust in his wrinkles.

For the second time, Ryan tried to speak. His voice was more of a croak than a wheeze now, and he watched the old man rise slowly to his feet and walk over to him.

Ryan wanted to ask the old man who he was, but he could not.

The *curandero* stopped at the edge of the shadow. He had managed to rig a crude shade with dried sticks and some of the cloth from Ryan's own shirt. He couldn't move Ryan; he wasn't strong enough, and besides, there was great danger in moving him. He moistened the cloth and put it to Ryan's mouth.

This time, Ryan was able to suck it greedily.

Ryan never did learn the old man's name.

Days passed, and the *curandero* gave him water as he needed it and eventually began to feed him. He began to cover Ryan's body with oils and poultices, and when Ryan was strong enough the *curandero* brewed up a batch of *pulque* from the cactus and got ready to do something about Ryan's arm.

It took Ryan awhile to get drunk enough, but when he got to the stage where he was seeing two of the old man and everything else around him, the *curandero* gave him a stick to bite on. Ryan clamped his teeth around it and felt his teeth sink into the wood.

The old man put his hands on Ryan's arm and Ryan bit harder. He knew what was coming, and even though the old man had done no more than touch him the pain rippled through him and caused his eyes to water. The *pulque* wasn't going to be enough.

The old man didn't waste time with hesitant motions. He had studied Ryan's arm and knew that while he could fix the breaks—he thought there were two—there was nothing he could do about the other damage, the damage done by the bullets.

When he snapped the first break into place, Ryan bit almost all the way through the stick. Then he passed out.

When he woke up, the old man gave him some more *pulque*, which helped a little. His arm didn't hurt as much as he had thought it might, and the pain in the rest of his body seemed to have lessened slightly. For the first time, Ryan began to think about whether he would live or die. For the first time, it began to make a difference to him.

Ryan didn't know it then, but the worst was yet to come, not from the pain, but from something different; not from pain, but from the lack of it.

It happened after what Ryan thought must have been nine days. He was never sure of the time, because he seemed to slip into and out of consciousness so often that he couldn't keep up accurately. But nine days seemed about right.

He had tried several times to talk to the old man. He knew a little bit of Spanish, and the old man also knew a few words, but Ryan was never sure they understood each other even remotely. He couldn't really tell the old man what he wanted. He wasn't even sure he could thank him.

What he wanted was to stand up.

He had thought about it for a day or two, but it hadn't seemed worth the effort. Maybe he had even been afraid of the pain it would cause, since for a day or so he had begun to feel much better. The torn and bleeding places on his body were healing, and his arm was on the mend. Standing would be a risk. He didn't want to jar anything around, didn't want to start up the pain again.

The old man moved him a little each day. Not much, just enough to change his position ever so slightly, to make sure he was lying on a somewhat different area of his skin. But he never tried to help Ryan sit up, much less stand.

Ryan was not a man accustomed to lying down. He was not accustomed to doing nothing. Even when he felt poorly he had always been up and about, doing whatever had to be done. He didn't want to change now; that would be too much like letting the pain get the better of him.

So he decided to stand up. First he would sit, and then he would stand. It seemed easy enough, when he was thinking about it.

That was the day he found out he couldn't move his legs.

It was getting on toward late afternoon when Ryan got back to the shack. His talk with Billy Kane had left him unsatisfied, and he didn't know what to do about it. There was something very convincing in Billy's statement that he hadn't killed Sally Ryan.

He remembered how Billy had been that night at the grove, how he had fired into the ground, and how he had stood so hesitantly before doing even that.

Billy had been scared that night. His voice had been as shaky as his hand. Ryan found it hard to believe that Billy was a killer, even the killer of a woman.

Ryan fed the bay and went inside. There were some tomatoes and peaches in the cans on the shelves. He could eat that and make some coffee afterward. He was hungry, but that would satisfy him. He wasn't ready to go to the cafe yet, and maybe he would never be.

He opened the cans and ate absently, his mind on other things. As he drank the juice out of the peach can, he thought about what Sheriff Bass had said: "They always confess in the end."

Ryan didn't think Billy would confess.

There was something else that Bass had said: "He's soft inside as anybody I ever saw."

Ryan thought that was true. No matter what kind of family Billy had, no matter what kind of man Kane was, Billy was soft. Too soft for killing. Ryan was sure of it.

So what did that mean? It meant that they were going to hang the wrong man. They were going to hang a man for a murder he didn't commit.

Ryan had ridden back to Tularosa for three reasons. One of them had been to see Billy Kane hang. When he read the news about his sister's death, he knew it was time to get back. There had been no reason for him not to believe the story about Billy Kane. It all seemed right and logical.

He thought about the other two reasons he had ridden back to Tularosa. To settle things with Kane, and to settle things with Virginia Burley. He felt no strong urge to do either now. What he felt mostly was a desire to let it all go, to get back on the bay horse and ride away. The direction wouldn't matter, as long as the road led away from where he was. Then he could lose himself again, the way he had been lost for the past few years.

He looked around the shack, at its bare walls of unpainted wood, its scarcely stocked shelves, its single window. His sister had died here in a struggle with her murderer, but it was nothing he could feel.

He got up from the table and went to the window. All the land that he could see had been his once, but now it was Kane's. The thought should have made him boil, but it hardly affected him at all.

It was getting dark now, and shadows were gathering among the trees. They would have finished Billy Kane's gallows by now, letting it sit for all the town to see and wonder at before the hanging on Saturday. If they hanged the wrong man, hardly anyone in the crowd would care. Most of them wouldn't even want to change things if they could. After all, it wasn't every day you got to see someone hang, much less one of the Kanes.

Ryan felt the lethargy getting the best of him, knowing that what he really wanted to do was lie on a cot and forget it all: Sally, Billy, Kane, Virginia Burley. Just put them all behind him and ride on.

But at the same time, he knew he couldn't. There was enough of the old Ryan left inside him to make that impossible. Whatever there was that hadn't been shot out, beaten out, and dragged out that night at Shatter's Grove was still strong enough to whisper in Ryan's mind and tell him that he had to do the right thing.

He turned from the window and went outside for his horse.


Pat Congrady lived above his store, and Ryan could see a faint light in the window. He tied his horse at the rail and climbed the wooden stairs on the outside of the building.

There was a narrow landing at the top of the stairs, and Ryan stood on it as he knocked on the door. He was sure that Congrady had heard his boots on the steps and would be wondering who would come calling after dark.

The door swung open. Congrady stood there looking out. The light from the room was too dim to illuminate the landing, and at first Congrady had no idea who was standing there.

"Who . . .?" he said, squinting his eyes.

"Ryan," Ryan told him.

"Ryan?" Congrady took a step forward. "You sonofa . . ." He caught himself before he finished the phrase, but his temper was flaring. He always lived up to the cliche about people with red hair.

"What are you doing here?" Congrady said. "It's too late now. Too late for Sally, and too late for you. I don't know what you're doing at my door, but you can leave right now. Leave, or by God I'll kick you down the stairs."

Ryan didn't move. "You probably could. I won't try to stop you. But I think we need to talk."

"I don't have anything to say to you, Ryan." Congrady's voice was husky with suppressed emotion. "I thought you were a man once, but you ran like a yellow dog. I don't have anything to say to someone who runs and leaves his sister. Leaves her to die."

Congrady bit his last words off sharply and stepped back into his room, swinging the door shut after him.

Ryan stepped forward and put his right hand on the door. "I don't blame you for the way you feel," he said. "But we still have to talk. I don't think Billy Kane killed Sally."

The rage seemed to drain out of Congrady like water from a leaky trough. "What?" he said.

"They're going to hang Billy for something he didn't do."

"How do you know?"

"I'm not sure. That's what I need to talk to you about."

Congrady sighed and opened the door. "All right," he said. "You might as well come in."

# Chapter Six

Kane's fat fingers twisted themselves together. In the lamplight they were even more pale than usual. McGee could hardly take his eyes off them. He and Barson sat in front of the desk in Kane's office and listened to their boss talk.

"All right," Kane was saying. "So he *is* back."

McGee wanted to say I told you so, but he didn't.

Barson couldn't resist. "Maybe it's just his ghost," he said.

Kane unclasped his hands and put them flat on the desk, staring straight at Barson. He didn't say anything, just stared.

Barson met his eyes for a few seconds. Then his gaze slipped down to the floor and skittered around the room.

"Sheriff Bass thinks he came back for the hangin'," McGee said, trying to break the tension.

"There won't be a hanging," Kane said. "I thought I told you that."

"Yeah, that's right. Sure," McGee said.

At that moment, Martin Long slipped into the room. He

entered so quietly that McGee didn't even know he was there until he had walked all the way to the desk.

"Well?" Kane said.

"He's stayin' at the shack," Long said. "Or somebody is. It's been cleaned up."

"But he's not there now?"

"Nobody's there now. I went in and checked." Long looked hurt. "If he'd been there, I'd of done something about him. You know that."

"Maybe you wouldn't be able to," Barson said. He had recovered some of his bravado.

"I could do it," Long said.

"Don't be so sure," Kane said. "You might recall a time when every one of us tried. And apparently failed."

"I guess so," Long said.

"No guessing is necessary now," Kane said. "Sit down, Long."

Long lowered his thin frame into a chair. His mouth was compressed into a thin line.

"Now," Kane said, "we have to decide what to do about Mr. Ryan. It seems certain that he has returned for more than a hanging." He glared at McGee as he spoke. "And all of you can guess what else has brought him back here, though you might wonder why he waited so long."

McGee felt the pain in his missing finger again and reached to massage it before he remembered.

"Hell," Barson said. "He wants a fight, we'll give him one. We got the best of him once, and we can do it again."

"We got the best of him, did we?" Kane said.

"Well, sure we did. We beat him half to death and that horse must of drug him twenty miles. What kind of a shape do you think that left him in?"

"It left him alive," Kane said. He leaned back in his chair and his face was in shadow. He looked like a huge headless blob of clothed flesh. Then he leaned forward again and the lamplight caught his eyes, which shone for just a second like the eyes of an animal, red in the whiteness of his face.

"It left him alive," he repeated, "and that was a mistake. If Billy had only—" He cut off his sentence. He didn't want to pursue that train of thought. Billy's actions on that night still rankled him. "Never mind that. We won't make the same mistake again. This time, we'll kill him. This time, we won't play around with him first."

"When?" Long said. He was ready now.

Barson nodded. He was ready, too.

McGee's finger hurt, and what he wished was that he could be somewhere else. He wasn't ready now, and he wasn't sure he'd ever be ready for Ryan again. There was something spooky about him coming back right at this time, and there was even something spooky in what Barson had said about maybe it was Ryan's ghost. It wasn't that McGee believed in ghosts, exactly, but his finger hurt him, didn't it? And that was a ghost, wasn't it?

"We'll take him later," Kane said. "He's not there now, anyway, and we've got other things to do, like getting Billy out of that jail. We don't want to stir things up too much before we take care of that."

McGee relaxed a little. That meant he didn't have to worry about Ryan for a day or so, at least. They weren't going to break Billy out until the next night.

"McGee went down to the jail today," Kane said. "He was doing his duty as a good citizen of the community, letting the officials of the law know about a suspicious stranger in town. Maybe he learned something that could be of use to us."

McGee frowned. He hadn't expected to be asked anything about his visit to the jail. He hadn't been looking around for anything out of the ordinary.

When McGee hesitated, Kane said, "Come, come, McGee. Surely you observed something while you were there. For example, how many officers were on duty?"

That was something that McGee remembered. "There were just two of them," he said. "One outside and one inside."

"Good," Kane said. "And that means there must be at least one more, back in the cells."

"I guess," McGee said. "They didn't let me back there."

"We've all seen that jail," Barson said. "Hell, I've even spent a few nights there myself. We could bust it down with a hammer, and if those three officers are just Bass, Higby, and Meadows, we can take care of them without any trouble at all."

"Of course," Kane said. "But you're forgetting one thing."

"What's that?" Barson said.

"Billy's in that jail," Kane said. "And if anything happens to him, I'll kill the rest of you myself." The lamplight struck his eyes again, and he smiled.

Ryan was uncomfortable in Congrady's room. It reminded him more of a woman's room than a man's, with frilly seat covers on the two chairs and a doily under the table lamp. There was a shelf of books, too, more books than Ryan had ever seen in one room.

It wasn't that Ryan couldn't read. He had read the Bible and *Pilgrim's Progress* and some book by a man named Cooper that told about a white man who had been raised by Indians and some of his adventures. But Congrady had all kinds of books. There must have been at least thirty of them.

Congrady was just as uncomfortable as Ryan, but for different reasons. He meant what he had said earlier. He would like to kick Ryan down the stairs. To him, Ryan was a man who had run out on his sister and left her to the mercy of Kane. And, as it turned out, to no mercy at all, though Ryan would have had no way of knowing that.

At the same time, Congrady was curious. Why, after all this time, had Ryan returned? Congrady was both curious and a little worried. He had never known exactly what to make of Ryan in the first place. Ryan was the kind of man who wore a gun and knew how to use it, the kind of man who wasn't afraid to stand up to other men when he knew he was in the right. In fact, as far as Congrady knew, Ryan wasn't the kind of man to be afraid of anything. So why had he disappeared in the first place?

Congrady, on the other hand, was a man who, despite his red hair and his fiery temper, usually backed down quickly—just as he had done with Ryan at the door. He was quick to anger, but he was just as quick to avoid a fight, unless it was with someone like Billy Kane, someone who wasn't going to give much of a fight.

And Congrady had a storekeeper's mentality. He liked things orderly and in their places—axe handles with axe handles, three-penny nails with three-penny nails, shovels with shovels. He didn't understand a man who could just pick up and leave an untidy situation like the one Ryan had with Kane. Besides, Congrady liked working inside, wearing an apron to keep the grease off his clothes. He could do heavy lifting, and his hands weren't entirely smooth and free of calluses, but he had never wanted to work in the outdoors, riding a horse and working cattle.

Congrady offered Ryan a seat, and he lowered himself stiffly and gingerly into one of the frilly chairs. Congrady sat opposite him, and the two men looked at each other warily.

Ryan finally opened the conversation. "I understand that you're the one who found Sally's body."

Congrady sat almost as stiffly as Ryan. "That's true. Except I didn't really find it. Billy Kane was already there."

"But he was there all along."

"Right. He was there. All along."

"So you brought him in."

"Yes. I did. I brought him in." Congrady was tapping his foot nervously on the floor.

Ryan ignored the tapping. "I hear he was beaten up pretty bad."

Congrady pushed himself out of the chair. "I was angry. I should have killed him." He wiped a hand over his face. "You don't know what it was like. He was just standing there, and Sally's body was on the floor. There was blood . . ."

"I guess I know what it looked like. I don't need you to tell me."

"I'm sorry," Congrady said.

"There's one thing that's been bothering me," Ryan said.

Congrady sat back down. "What's that?"

"Has anyone asked Billy what he was doing there in the first place?"

Congrady looked absently around the room, as if he didn't want to meet Ryan's eyes. "I . . . guess most people already knew."

Ryan shifted in the chair, trying to get into a comfortable position. He couldn't. "They knew why he was there?"

"Yes. They knew."

"Nobody's told *me,*" Ryan said.

"Did you ask the sheriff?"

"No."

"He could tell you." Congrady was plainly uncomfortable.

"You're the one I'm asking."

"Why me?" Congrady's tone was aggrieved.

"Because I know you. Or I knew you. You were courting Sally. You should have known her better than anyone."

"Maybe I did," Congrady said. "But it's not something I like to talk about."

"What's not?"

"Her and Billy Kane."

Ryan felt a little stirring inside him. It wasn't interest, exactly, but it was as close to interest as he'd felt in a long time. "Her and Billy Kane? What about them?"

"Everybody in town knew," Congrady said. "Billy . . . well, Billy took a liking to her. He felt bad about the way she'd been treated by his brother. And by her brother," he added, looking sharply at Ryan.

Ryan did not respond. He sat stiffly in the chair, his eyes on Congrady's face.

"Anyway," Congrady went on, "Billy took to visiting Sally whenever he could. He tried to keep it a secret, but of course I knew. Sally told me. Eventually the whole town knew."

"How?"

"Well, they kept seeing him heading out that way. There was

only one reason to be heading out to that shack, and that was to see Sally Ryan. People talked about it."

Ryan could believe that. Tularosa was like any other town. "Did his brother know?" he said.

Congrady shook his head. "I don't think so. Who was going to tell him? Billy? Not likely. And you might not know it, but Kane doesn't have a whole lot of friends in this town."

"If Billy felt sorry for her, why did he kill her?"

"Ask him," Congrady said. "He's the one that would know."

"He says he didn't do it."

"You didn't expect him to admit it, did you?"

"You're the one who said to ask him," Ryan reminded him. "Was there anybody else who might want to kill Sally?"

"No. She was a wonderful girl, no matter what—" Congrady stopped and let his eyes travel around the room again.

"I think you better finish saying whatever it was you had on your mind," Ryan said.

"It's just Kane," Congrady said. "It didn't mean anything. He tried to start stories around town about Sally, about how she was nothing but a . . . a prostitute."

The stirring in Ryan was a little stronger now. He sat forward in the chair. "Kane said that?"

"Not Kane. You know that he'd never do something like that himself. But he got people to do it. Long. Barson. You know."

Ryan knew, all right. "He was trying to influence the jury, I expect."

"It didn't work, though," Congrady said. "People knew where the stories were coming from."

"You still haven't told me why Billy killed her."

"How should I know? Maybe it was because she wasn't what the stories said she was. She was going to marry me. She didn't have time for Billy Kane."

Ryan had never been overly fond of Congrady, even before Sally's death, but Sally had thought of him as a strong man, one who knew what he wanted to accomplish in life and one who would make a good family man. Now Ryan wondered just how much help Congrady had been to Sally in the last few years, especially in the days when she was having to deal with Kane. Had he been any help at all?

It wasn't a question he was ready to explore. "So the feeling is that Billy Kane went out to the shack and killed Sally out of jealousy, or something like that?"

Congrady nodded agreement. "Something like that," he repeated.

"And nobody else had any reason to be there before Billy?"

"Who would want to? There was nothing there to steal. She didn't have anything left, thanks to—" Congrady cut himself off. "Anyway, she didn't have anything out there worth stealing, and unless those rumors Kane started are true she didn't have a lot of visitors." Congrady's mouth twisted as he spoke the final sentence.

Ryan didn't let it bother him. He had known Sally too well to worry about such stories. It was just one more little item to add to Kane's list. Ryan wished that it bothered him more than it did. The old Ryan, the one that had existed before that night in Shatter's Grove, would already have ridden out to Kane's place and called him out, settled everything once and for all.

The new Ryan wasn't like that. Maybe he had lost more than he thought that night and the days and months afterward.

Or maybe it was something else. Maybe he had learned that life was too important to be given over to rushing into things. Maybe he had learned the value of patience.

He wasn't sure, and it wasn't something he wanted to talk over with Congrady. He didn't feel that he owed Congrady explanations of any kind, not for the way he felt now, or for the way he had left Sally.

Ryan got slowly out of the chair. It was the only way he *could* get out of a chair these days. "I guess you can't tell me any more, then."

Congrady stood up. "No. Billy did it, even if we don't know why. If he says different, then he's a liar. What else would you expect from a Kane?"

As Ryan walked back down the stairs, he thought about what Congrady had told him, which really didn't amount to much.

He wondered how Congrady had felt about those rumors, and he wondered just how far Congrady might go if he believed Billy Kane was making any headway with Sally.

What if Sally and Billy Kane had begun to develop some kind of relationship that threatened Pat Congrady? Sally had always been the kind of girl who liked to adopt stray dogs, of which there were always plenty in Tularosa. There had been a time, Ryan remembered, when there had been at least five of them living around the house.

Maybe Billy Kane was another stray that Sally had picked up. It wasn't in her to hold his brother's meanness against him.

And how would Pat Congrady have liked that?

# *Chapter Seven*

That night Ryan dreamed about the eagle.

He had dreamed of the eagle the first time after discovering that he couldn't move his legs, and at first the dream was always the same.

Ryan would be riding through desert country, and the dust would be heavy on his duster. He would have a three-day growth of beard, and his face would be caked with dust and the salt from his sweat. He would ride and ride, skirting cactus and stones, stopping once to fire his pistol at a rattler beside the trail.

Then through a haze of shimmering heat waves he would see the trading post in the distance. He always resisted the urge to spur up his horse, since he knew that the horse didn't have much more to give. They both needed water and food, but water most of all.

The trading post was almost falling down when he got there. The logs and wood were rotten and seemed to lean crazily one way or the other. The hitching rail crumbled in his hands when he tried to tie the horse's reins to it.

When he went inside, there was no one there. He called out, and his voice was hollow in the echoing room. There were cans on the shelves, but they were dusty, as if no one had handled them for days. Dust sifted down on his hat from the ceiling.

He knew there would be a well out back, however. There had to be, or there would be no trading post there in the first place. When he turned to go outside and look for it, he saw the eagle.

It was in a wooden cage about four feet long, three feet wide, and not much taller than the eagle himself. The bird would walk the length of the cage, turn, and walk back the other way.

Turn again.

Walk back.

Turn.

Walk.

The eagle's feathers on each side were worn away from brushing the sides of the cage in his walking and turning.

Ryan was a man who could stand his own pain, but he was sensitive to the pain of others, and to see an eagle caged like that, his restless spirit confined to the walking and turning, almost made Ryan ill.

He called out again, and again there was no answer.

He walked over to the cage. There was a door on one end, hinged with leather and tied shut with a buckskin thong.

Ryan picked up the cage and carried it outside. The sun had retreated behind a cloud, and a northerly wind was kicking up the dust.

He set the cage on the ground and untied the thong, then pulled open the door.

The eagle paced toward the opening. When he reached it, he didn't even pause.

He turned.

And walked back the other way.

When he reached the other end of the cage, he turned once more, walked the exact number of paces that he always walked, came to the open door, and turned.

Walked back.

Turned.

Ryan woke up soaked in sweat, and the next day he tried to tell the old man about the dream. The Indian listened, and he seemed to understand at least part of it, the part about the eagle, but Ryan wasn't sure if the part about the cage was clear or not. The whole thing seemed to excite the old man quite a bit, but Ryan wasn't ever able to figure out exactly why.

The dream was different now. It was longer. Ryan could remember just when it had changed. It was after the old man had made him walk again.

It had taken a long time—months, Ryan thought, but he was never quite sure. It could have been weeks, or it could have been a year.

The old man had worked on Ryan's legs and back every day after Ryan made him understand that he couldn't walk. He had turned Ryan over and massaged his spine. He had exercised Ryan's legs every day, manipulating them up and down in walking motions. Finally the feeling had returned to them, and the old man had made some kind of brace for Ryan's back.

It was made mostly of leather, which had come from God knows where. Ryan never found out. It reminded Ryan of nothing so much as a corset of the kind he had seen drawn in a catalogue once, but he put it on, and the Indian laced it up.

Then the *curandero* bent down and put Ryan's right arm over his shoulder and stood up. Ryan thought of himself as a big man, and he would have thought it would have been impossible for a frail figure like the Indian to move him at all. Nevertheless, he came up easily and stood on his feet for the first time in so long that he couldn't remember.

The old man spoke to him, urging him to take a step, or so Ryan supposed.

He tried it, and his knees buckled.

The old man held him up. Either Ryan had lost more weight than he knew, or the old man was very strong.

Ryan tried again. This time he made it without folding. He was still in pain, but at least he knew that he would be able to walk.

The old man worked with him every day after that.

His arm, the left one, had healed as well. It would never be much use to him; he could tell that by looking. The elbow looked like two elbows now, and neither one seemed to be in the right place. It looked as if two knobs were attached to his arm under the skin. He could raise his arm, but only very slowly and with great difficulty and pain. Somehow he knew that it would never get much better.

The fingers of his left hand were virtually frozen in place. He could brace things with it, but it was almost impossible for him to grip them. The hand seemed to be cold all the time.

He still dreamed the dream, but now the eagle left the cage. After turning from the exit three times, the bird paused and looked out, as if noticing for the first time that the wooden bars were gone. Then it stuck its head out and looked from side to side. With another step, its body followed along, and the bird was out.

And there it sat, never moving, as the dusty wind ruffled its feathers and as Ryan stood there and yelled at it, flapping his right arm at his side, trying to make it fly.

But it never did, and Ryan still woke up sweating.

The next day, Ryan went back into town. He passed by the pile of tin cans on that side of town and wondered how Tularosa or any Western town would look in twenty years. They would be able to build the houses out of tin cans.

He rode past the jail and the gallows. It was sturdy and solid-looking, with a lot of new wood mixed in with some old boards that had been scavenged from some place or another. It would do the job, but Ryan just couldn't believe Kane would let the hanging take place, especially not with Billy protesting his innocence. Ryan was surprised Kane hadn't tried to break him out already.

Ryan looked down the street in front of him. It was still early, but the town was awake and busy. There were a lot of wagons, a lot of women and children around. Ryan was sure that most of them were from out of town, having come in early for the hanging. There would be a real crowd by the next day, and a festive atmosphere. Picnic lunches, laughing, joking, just like a big party.

A necktie party, they would call it, a good time for everyone, if Kane didn't spoil it. Ryan thought he would try.

He felt that flicker in him again, something like interest, but it wasn't any stronger than it had been the night before.

Billy Kane wasn't really on his mind this morning. He had decided to eat breakfast in town, to see if the food had changed any at Wilson's. Maybe to see what else had changed.

The cafe was crowded, and there was lots of talk. The crowd was mostly men, men in bib overalls, jeans, and boots. Cowboys and a few farmers, though the land around Tularosa didn't lend itself much to farming. The talk was mostly about the hanging.

Ryan overheard some of it.

". . . damned Kanes deserve what they get . . ."

". . . hangin's too good if you ask . . ."

". . . never would of happened if . . ."

The talk shut down when the men looked up and saw Ryan standing in the doorway. To most of them he was a stranger, and the scar on his face, the way he stood, the way he held his arm, would have rendered him unfamiliar to most of the others.

Still, one or two of them knew him and recognized him. They leaned over and spoke to their neighbors in whispers, and the general buzz of talk began again.

None of it bothered Ryan. He had long ago ceased to care very much about the opinions of others. He looked around for a table that was vacant. There was only one, and he took it. Somehow he didn't think anyone would be joining him.

He sat and looked around the room for Virginia Burley. She generally waited on the tables herself now, and collected for the meals. There had been a time, Ryan recalled, when she had done most of the cooking, too, but she had finally been able to hire someone for that job.

The interest that had turned to Ryan when he entered had all subsided. Those who knew who he was had told others, and the news had been passed around to others, but no one was going to say too much about it. Not with Ryan in the room. After he left, it would be different, but people still recalled the way he had been, the way he could use a gun and the way he wasn't afraid of any man. He might look changed, but you couldn't always tell what a man was by the way he looked. So the talk turned back to the hanging and to other things.

Virginia Burley came through the door from the kitchen. She was carrying a thick white plate full of eggs and bacon and grits in one hand and an equally thick mug of steaming coffee in the other.

Her dark hair was pinned up, but a few strands of it were straggling loose at the back and hung down her neck. Her white skin was flushed from the heat of the kitchen.

When she saw Ryan, the flush deepened. She had not known how she would respond if he showed up, and now there he was, sitting calmly at a table and watching her. She was suddenly conscious of her every movement, and the plate and mug felt as if they weighed ten pounds each.

She managed to deliver them to the proper table, setting them down carefully and spilling only a drop or two of the coffee. The hot drops hit her hand, but she didn't notice.

She collected her thoughts and walked over to the table where Ryan sat. There was a lull in the talk as men watched to see what would happen, but she didn't notice that, either.

Ryan watched her come toward him. He hadn't known how he would react, any more than she had. He had thought about her for years, about what he would do or say when—if—he ever saw her again, and he suddenly realized that she was one of the reasons he had never returned to Tularosa.

By the time he had recovered enough to walk, much less ride, it was far too late to do anything about his land or his sister. He knew that Kane would have long since taken control, and he was sure that Sally could fend for herself on whatever was left. She was a Ryan, and she was tough. It turned out that he had been wrong about that, but he didn't blame himself. It was beginning to look as if her death was entirely unconnected to his troubles with Kane.

And whatever had happened inside of him had burned away the desire for revenge. There had been a time when he would have ridden remorselessly after Kane and McGee and Barson and Long. Even after Billy. And he would not have rested until they were dead, or he was. Even revenge didn't interest him now, however.

So there was no real reason for him to ride back to Tularosa, just as there had been no reason for him not to. Yes, he had wanted to see Billy Kane hang, and he had wanted, in a vague way, to settle things with Billy's brother and with Virginia Burley, but those things didn't really matter to him.

Somehow he no longer really cared.

Even looking at Virginia didn't change that. He had thought he might feel a great surge of hatred or disgust, but he felt neither. On the other hand, he felt no return of the desire or love, or whatever it had been that had once motivated him where she was concerned.

He felt only that tiny stirring within him, of interest, curiosity, whatever it was. And it still wasn't strong enough to move him.

She stood awkwardly at his table, the flush still on her face. "Hello, Ryan," she said. Her voice was low and husky, but it had always been that way. "I wasn't sure you'd come in."

"I wanted breakfast," he said. "I never was much of a cook."

"I remember," she said, and at once she was flooded with other memories: she and Ryan in the wagon in the evenings, the way his hand would brush hers, the way something in her seemed to melt when he looked at her.

She told herself to stop it. She had done what she had done, and there was no changing it. She had wanted her independence, and she had gotten it the only way she knew how. But she hadn't realized what it would cost her, and what it would cost Ryan.

She looked at his face, trying not to stare at the scar. She saw the way he held his arm, the stiff way he sat in the chair, and resisted the desire to turn her head.

"I'd like bacon and eggs," Ryan said. "No grits."

"I . . . I'll bring them," she said, and turned back toward the kitchen.

As she walked away, Ryan thought of the way she had looked at him. He hadn't given much thought to his appearance in the past few years, but he realized how it must affect people.

He took off his hat and put it on one of the other chairs at the table. No one looked at him directly, but he thought they were assessing his face. Most of them still had their hats on, Eastern ideas of politeness not having much influence on them.

He didn't know how he had gotten the scar. His face had hurt, along with all the rest of him, and the old man who had found him hadn't been carrying any mirrors, so Ryan hadn't done much looking. Probably scraped his face on a rock while the horse was dragging him along, Ryan thought. He really didn't care; his face had been the least of his problems.

Virginia returned with the plate of bacon and eggs, along with a cup of coffee that Ryan hadn't asked for. Coffee came with everything.

She set the plate and cup on the table. "I want to talk to you," she said. She had come to the decision somewhere between the kitchen and his table. She wasn't sure why she had made it. Maybe just seeing him there, seeing that he was really alive, was what had decided her.

"All right," he said. "Talk." He put copious amounts of salt and pepper on his eggs, sprinkling the condiments from shakers that sat on the table. Then he put a fork into the eggs and started eating.

She watched him eat for a second or two. "I don't mean right now," she said. "Later."

Ryan finished chewing the mouthful of eggs. They were scrambled just right, not too soft, not too hard. "How much later?" He wasn't sure that he had any plans for the day, but he didn't want to tie himself down.

"About ten o'clock," she said. "There shouldn't be anyone here then. Could you come back?"

He could. The question was, did he want to? He thought it over, eating another bite of the eggs and taking a taste of the bacon. The bacon was a little limp.

The more he thought about it, the more he realized that he did want to talk to Virginia Burley. His curiosity had not entirely disappeared. He wanted to know why she had not sent the sheriff that night, and this would be his chance to ask her.

It wasn't that he held it against her; it wasn't even that he wanted to do anything about it. In his mild way, he simply wanted to know.

"I'll be here," he said.

The corners of her mouth turned up slightly in what might have been a smile. "Good."

She almost started to say more, but she didn't. She turned and went to pick up another order from the kitchen.

Ryan ate his bacon and eggs, taking an occasional drink from the thick coffee mug. He didn't like to drink coffee until it got almost cool. It had a tendency to burn the roof of his mouth. He had known people who could practically drink it right out of the pot, but he wasn't one of them.

As he ate, he watched Virginia move around the room full of tables, taking orders, carrying plates, occasionally talking to one or another of the men that she knew.

He wondered what she wanted to tell him. That she was sorry? That she had missed him? That the horse had thrown a shoe, or the wagon had thrown a wheel? Maybe she had gotten lost, or maybe the sheriff had been out of town. There were any number of explanations for what had happened, and Ryan had thought of them all at one time or another as he lay there being taken care of by an old Indian whose name he didn't even know, wondering if he would ever be able to ride or even walk again.

Strangely enough, he had never blamed her for what had happened. He was not a man to put the blame on others. It had been his own fault for being careless, and Kane's fault for being greedy. Whatever had happened, none of it could be traced to Virginia.

Maybe she felt guilty now; maybe she wanted to clear her conscience.

Ryan sipped his coffee slowly. It was almost cold now, the way he liked it. It was only a few hours until ten o'clock. He could wait.

He was good at waiting.

# Chapter Eight

The *curandero* had taught him patience, among other things.

While Ryan was healing, the old man squatted on his haunches during the day, his shoulders hunched like a buzzard's. Sometimes he slept. Sometimes Ryan could feel his eyes on him even though the old man appeared to be sleeping.

He never seemed to hurry, never seemed to have anything else in mind besides helping Ryan. He helped as Ryan struggled to walk. He put the herbal oils on Ryan's wounds. He talked, if Ryan wanted to talk, despite the fact that neither could understand the other.

When Ryan talked about the dream, all he could understand of the old man's Spanish was *"tu espíritu,"* your spirit.

Ryan wasn't even sure he understood that. He understood the words, that is, but not what was behind them, unless it had to do with something mystical. That was all right for Indians, but Ryan didn't believe in any of that himself.

Eventually, with a lot of pain, a lot of effort, and a lot of help from the *curandero*, Ryan began walking more and more. "I'll never be able to chase jackrabbits again," he said.

The old man said something in reply, and for once Ryan got it. "Chase, yes. Catch, no."

They both laughed, and Ryan walked nearly a mile that day.

By then he was able to help the Indian build a better shelter. There wasn't much wood, but they were able to walk to a fair-sized boulder and put together a sort of lean-to against it. It was a big help in the sun, and even in the occasional rain shower.

Ryan was eating more, too. Somehow the old man managed to provide rabbits and birds, along with an armadillo or two. Ryan was not particularly fond of armadillo, but he ate it.

Now and then he would wonder how far they might be from a town, and how soon he would be able to go to one again, but when he thought about the stiff and hobbling way he walked, the way he had to carry his left arm useless at his side, he put the idea of town away for a while.

The Indian usually hunted late in the afternoon or night. He seldom went anywhere at all during the day. Then once at dusk he disappeared into the gloom and did not return for two days. Ryan worried that he might be dead or that he might have broken a leg and been unable to come back.

He needn't have worried. The old man showed up carrying a roll of clothing, more or less in Ryan's size, and in the middle of the roll was a leather double-loop holster and a Colt's Peacemaker .45 in the short-barreled model. The gun belt was filled with shiny cartridges.

"How?" Ryan said.

The old man didn't say anything. He just dug into his black shirt and pulled out a small, worn leather pouch tied with a draw-string. He loosened the string and dumped the contents of the pouch into his wrinkled hand, a hand almost as leathery as the pouch.

Ryan saw that he was holding several very small particles of gold. Was the Indian finding that at night, too, along with the small game? It was one more thing about him that Ryan never learned.

The old man poured the gold back into the pouch and drew the string tight by holding one end in his hand and the other in the yellowed stubs of his teeth.

The gun did not look new, and Ryan wondered who the old man had bought it from. He didn't talk. His next question was more complicated than that, though it consisted of only one word.

"Why?"

The Indian merely smiled and shook his head.

It was awhile before Ryan got around to wearing the clothes, and even longer before he strapped on the gun.

By then, he'd forgotten how to hurry.

Ryan walked around Tularosa, looking at the people, the women in their fancy dresses and bonnets, the children in their Sunday best, all come to see Billy Kane's neck stretched.

Everyone seemed in a fine mood, so Ryan didn't spoil things by going to the jail. He was fairly certain Billy Kane wasn't nearly as happy about his date with the gallows as everyone else seemed to be.

At ten o'clock, he went back to Wilson's. As Virginia had said, there was no one there. The breakfast eaters had long since left, and the lunch crowd would not be there for an hour or so.

Virginia was sitting at a table near the door. She had put up her hair again, and washed her face. She sat calmly, her hands clasped in front of her.

"Hello," she said when Ryan stepped through the door.

"Hello," he replied. This time he took his hat off at once. Then he walked over to the table. "You wanted to talk?"

"Please," she said. "Sit down."

Ryan pulled out the chair opposite her. Its legs scraped across the wooden floor. He eased himself down.

Neither knew how to begin the conversation. Ryan watched her eyes, the way her breasts pushed against the smooth front of the blue dress. She had been wearing an apron earlier, but it was gone now.

"There are some things I want to tell you," she said after a few silent moments had passed.

"You don't owe me anything," he said.

"This doesn't have anything to do with . . . us," she said. "It's about Billy Kane, and your sister."

Ryan waited to hear what she had to say.

"I hear a lot of things in a place like this," she told him, looking around the room at the empty tables and chairs. "Sooner or later most of the single men in town come in here to eat, and they aren't always careful about what they say."

That was an interesting fact, Ryan supposed, but he didn't see where it was leading. He remained silent.

"You're not making this easy," she said, twisting her fingers together.

"I didn't know I was supposed to."

"You're not. It's just that . . . never mind. I was going to tell you something. I don't think Billy Kane killed Sally. Most people don't think so."

"The jury did."

"That's what they said. I think they just hate the Kanes. Most of the people who come in here feel the same way. They aren't sorry Billy's going to hang. As far as they're concerned, he deserves it for being a member of his family. But they don't really believe he did it."

Ryan didn't believe it, either, and he didn't think the sheriff did. "What am I supposed to do?"

"I . . . don't know. I thought . . ." She stopped for a minute. "I'm not sure what I thought." She looked at Ryan almost resentfully.

"You want me to tell you what you thought?" he said. "You thought that I'd do something about it. You had some idea that in the interests of justice I'd step in and try to make things right."

Even saying it made him feel tired, but she looked at him directly for the first time, turned her dark eyes fully on his. "Yes, I guess that's pretty much what I thought."

"There was a time I might have," he said. "Things change, though. I've changed."

"I don't believe that."

"That doesn't make it a lie."

Their eyes locked and they sat for several minutes saying nothing. The time seemed to drag by, but neither one was inclined to break the silence.

After a while, Virginia said, "Kane won't let them do it, anyway."

"I'd wondered about that," Ryan said. "He's not the kind to sit by and let his brother die, no matter what else he might do."

"Long and Barson eat in here occasionally. McGee, too," she said.

"And?"

"Something will happen tonight. I'm not sure what."

"Have you told the sheriff?"

"No."

"And you want me to?"

"If you would."

Ryan didn't want to get involved, but he said he would tell Bass. "That's all you had to say?"

"Yes. That's all."

Ryan stood awkwardly to leave. Moving around didn't hurt him anymore; it just wasn't as easy to do as it had once been.

She watched him rise, and something twisted in her like a knife in her heart. "Wait."

Ryan put a hand on the back of the chair to steady himself.

"Don't go yet," she said. "There's something else I have to tell you."

He sat back down in the chair then, and she told him the whole thing, about her husband and her brother, her fears of being dependent and how Kane had played on them, how she had not sent the sheriff to Shatter's Grove because of what Kane had promised her.

When she had finished, tears were running down her cheeks, but she was not sobbing. Her voice was steady. "You deserved to know," she said. "Whatever changed you, whatever has happened to you, is my fault. I don't think Billy Kane should die for something I did."

It was not her fault, but there was no way Ryan could explain that to her, no way he could tell her that he was not letting Billy hang because of revenge, but simply because he didn't care.

Besides, something was beginning to move in him because of what she had said. The flickers of interest were beginning to coalesce into a fire, a fire that was starting to burn because of Kane.

It wasn't even that Kane had taken his land and hounded his sister, though that was part of it.

It was the way that Kane had used a weakness within Virginia Burley to get at Ryan. One part of Ryan even resented the fact that Kane had been able to see the weakness that Ryan had never seen.

As Ryan thought about it, he realized that was typical of Kane's methods. Everyone had a weakness, if you could only find it. And if you could exploit that weakness, you could beat them.

He felt a twinge of guilt then, for the first time, about Sally. Maybe he had done too much for her, let her depend on him for too many things. In that way, he might have been unfair to her just as Virginia's husband and brother were. They had left her, through no fault of their own, just as he had left his sister. Virginia had managed to succeed where Sally had failed, but only by a form of treachery.

Ryan, who had lost all taste for personal vengeance, now felt that he wanted to get revenge for someone else: for Virginia Burley and for Sally Ryan. That revenge would not be served if Billy Kane died unjustly.

"You shouldn't worry about what you did," Ryan said. "It was what you had to do."

"No, I didn't. I know that now. You could have handled Kane, and you could have taken care of me."

"Don't say that." Ryan's voice was hard. "I never wanted to 'take care' of you or anybody, man or woman. You take care of yourself just fine."

Then Ryan smiled. "I have to admit, I wish you could have found some other way of taking care of yourself, but I don't blame you. Not a bit."

Virginia took a napkin from the table and dried her face. "I think you actually mean that."

"I do, but I don't like the way Kane used you. Or my sister. I may even do something about it."

"You said you'd changed. But you haven't."

"Maybe not. I thought I had. I could have been wrong."

Virginia smiled, too. "I hope you were. I liked the Ryan I knew." The smile vanished. "But not enough to . . ."

"Don't say it," Ryan told her. "You don't have to say anything. Whatever happened is over and done with. It was Kane. Not you."

Virginia wanted to agree with him, but she couldn't. She knew, she would always know, that it wasn't Kane's fault, as much as she might want it to be and wish it was. "It was me, too," she said.

Ryan reached across the table and touched her hand. "If it was, it doesn't matter," he said, and her tears started again.

Ryan pretended not to see. "If you hear so many things in here, who do people say killed Sally? They must have some idea."

He knew Tularosa. Everyone would have an idea, and most of them would want to talk about it sooner or later.

Virginia used the napkin again. "Some of them have mentioned Pat Congrady. They don't say his name loudly, though."

Ryan had already had the same thought. "Who else?"

"You know that nearly everyone knew about Billy and your sister?"

"Yes, and I've heard the rumors Kane started. I don't believe them."

"Neither does anyone else in town, but they're nasty rumors anyway. Billy was trying to keep his visits to Sally a secret from his brother. You know that Kane would never have permitted them if he had known."

Ryan nodded. "He wouldn't want any of us Ryans getting that

close to the Kanes. There would always be a chance of us getting the land back."

"That's true. And maybe he didn't know. He hardly ever leaves that house of his except for—" She stopped thinking about the last time she knew of Kane having left his house, three years before.

"I know why he leaves," Ryan said. "To take things."

"Yes." Her lips compressed into a thin line. "Anyway, he might not have known. But I'm sure that Barson and Long knew. I heard them talking about it one day in here."

"You think they might have done something about it on their own?"

"It's possible. I don't really know."

Ryan thought about it. "Why wouldn't they have told Kane about Billy and Sally?"

"They're just as afraid of him as everyone else in this town. They wouldn't have wanted to be the ones bringing the bad news to him. You know what happens to people who bring news like that."

"So they might have decided to take care of the problem without telling Kane. And afterward, when Billy got caught with the body, they couldn't say anything. He would have killed them."

Virginia nodded in agreement. "Or at least he would have turned them in, and they wouldn't have lasted as long as Billy. They would have been lynched. People here hate them as much as they hate Kane."

Ryan knew that was the truth. Barson, Long, and even McGee had pretty much had their way in Tularosa for years. They could get drunk and beat up farmers and cowhands, even shoot up the town, and no one would ever complain. Complaints would have brought retaliation much worse than whatever had happened at first. The only way they ever spent time in the local jail was if they were caught in the act, something that had only happened once or twice. And then no one was ever willing to come forward and make a real complaint, so they were out in a day or two.

Ryan didn't know about McGee, but he was certain that Long or Barson either one would be capable of murder, even the murder of a woman, without thinking twice.

"I'll see what I can do about all this," he said.

"I thought . . . I was *sure* you would. I'm glad you let me tell you. You were always easy to talk to."

Ryan didn't want the conversation to take a personal turn. He had been guiding it in a different direction all along because he didn't know where personal things might lead. He was feeling much more like his old self, but he was still uncertain about a lot of things, particularly his feelings about Virginia.

"I'll talk to the sheriff," he said. "I'm not sure what good it will do. Billy's been tried and convicted. The rope's waiting. There's not much Bass can do."

"At least you can try," she said. "I'd tell him myself, but I don't think he would put much stock in the word of a woman."

Ryan got up again. He didn't tell her that Bass had plenty of doubts of his own. He put on his hat. "I'll see what I can do," he said.

She watched him cross the room. "Come back again," she said as he went through the door.

He gave no sign that he had heard.

The full force of the heat and sun hit him as he stepped outside. The streets were less crowded now, but there was a small knot of men standing on the plank walk a few yards away.

When the men saw Ryan, they moved toward him. The news that he was back had spread around the town, and while many people considered that whatever he had been doing for the last few years was his own business, there are always a few who figure they know what a man's business is better than he does.

Ryan recognized several of the men. In the front of the group was George Maze, who ran the livery stable. Right behind him were Walt Albert and Jack Crabtree, followed by three others whose names Ryan couldn't recall. Albert, he remembered, taught in the one-room school outside of town and gave music lessons on the side. Crabtree worked for Maze and did most of the hard work—and the dirty work—at the stable.

Maze was the spokesman. "I'm George Maze," he said. "You remember me, Ryan?"

"I remember you. And Albert and Crabtree."

"Thought you might." Maze was wearing an old hat that sagged down around his face and head. His head bobbed as he talked. "I don't want to waste your time, but me and some of the boys wanted to have a little talk with you."

Ryan looked up at the perfectly blue sky and felt the sun burning through his shirt. "Go ahead and talk," he said.

"Well, it looks to some of us like you left town at a mighty funny time and came back the same way." Maze looked out from under his hat brim as defiantly as it was possible for him to look.

Ryan stared back at him, unable to see his eyes in the shadow of the hat brim. "What does that mean?" he said.

Albert spoke up hesitantly. He was basically a shy person who didn't know exactly what he was doing there. He had just gotten roped into the group because he had been standing in the mercantile store when they started talking about Ryan's unexpected return. "We're simply wondering why you chose this particular time to return," he said.

Ryan knew that people were naturally curious, and despite his reservations about Virginia Burley, he had admired her restraint in their conversation in the cafe. Never once had she asked him where he had been or why he had come back.

"Maybe I just wanted to," Ryan said.

Crabtree shoved forward belligerently. "That's a kind of a smart answer, if you ask me."

Ryan looked at him mildly. "I don't remember asking you."

"Now, now," Albert said. "All we want to do is assure ourselves that you haven't come back for some purpose that would be harmful to the town."

Ryan couldn't figure out what they were talking about. "Try making sense," he said.

"You know what we mean," Crabtree said. He was getting

more and more upset, clenching and unclenching his fists. Ryan remembered that he had more than once been fired by Maze for rough treatment of the animals they stabled. But he had always been rehired, since there was hardly anyone else who would do the work for the wages Maze paid.

"No," Ryan said. "I don't know what you mean."

"We mean we intend to see Billy Kane swinging at the end of a rope tomorrow," Maze said. "And you better not do anything about it. It was your sister he killed. Remember that."

Ryan didn't say anything. Did they really think he could forget who was dead?

"Yeah," Crabtree said. "Your sister. He probably raped her, too."

No one had as yet made that suggestion, and even Maze appeared a bit shocked at the blunt statement. He tried to cover it up. "We don't know that, but we do know he killed her. And we want to see him die for it. If that's what you came back here to see, fine."

Now Ryan knew what the problem was. They all remembered the old Ryan, the one who wouldn't have put up with the twisting of justice for any reason, and they had all heard the rumors about Billy Kane's innocence. What's more, they probably believed them. Otherwise they wouldn't be making such a point of warning Ryan off. They wanted Kane to die, guilty or not.

"That's what I came to see," Ryan said. It was the truth. He had changed his mind since coming, however, but only a few minutes before.

"Good," Maze said. "I guess that's it, then."

"You believe him?" Crabtree said. "Can't you see he's lyin'?"

The other five men had begun to move off. Crabtree stood his ground. "I say you're lyin'," he said.

It was the kind of insult that some men would have considered deadly. Ryan had been like that once, or nearly like that. He certainly would at least have flattened Crabtree with a hard right to the face.

Now he did nothing, except to stand his ground as Crabtree crowded up to him, bumping him with his chest. Crabtree smelled of the stables, of oats and corn and horse manure.

"You hear me, Ryan? I say you're a liar."

"I hear you." Ryan still didn't move.

Crabtree turned abruptly away. "I guess we don't have to worry about him, fellers," he said to the others. "I don't know where he's been, but it's flat turned him yeller."

The other men had been silent before, but now the silence was almost something you could feel in the air. They expected Ryan to draw, or to call Crabtree down.

He did neither; simply stood there, watching them.

Crabtree walked past the small group of men and on down the boardwalk.

After a minute, the others turned and followed.

# Chapter Nine

Ryan watched them go. Crabtree separated from the others, and Ryan saw him stop at the door of Pat Congrady's hardware store. Congrady came out and the two men talked for a minute, then Crabtree went inside. Ryan would have liked to know what they had to say to one another.

From the opposite side of the street, someone was watching Ryan. Three-finger Johnny McGee was sitting on another part of the walk today, still throwing his knife into the planks and watching the handle quiver as the blade sank solidly in. He hadn't been able to hear what was said, but he could tell that Crabtree and Ryan were not on the best of terms. He thought it was something the others should know about. He got to his feet and sidled off down the alley between two buildings to go and report to Kane.

Ryan meanwhile got his horse and rode to the jail. Meadows was more alert today, and Ryan took his holster and gun off without being asked. When he went inside, Bass was sitting with his boots up on his desk, smoking.

"I hear that Kane has something planned for tonight," Ryan said without preamble. "I thought you ought to know about it."

"I've been hearing that for a week," Bass said. "I'm not too worried about it. Like I said, there're three of us here, and we've all got guns." He put his boots on the floor and stood up, stretching.

"I imagine you're all getting pretty tired by now," Ryan said, watching him. "That might be what Kane is counting on."

"We can handle one more night."

"I also hear that a lot of folks around town think Billy probably didn't kill my sister."

"Yeah. That's too bad. But the jury thought otherwise, and the jury's decision is what I have to go by." Bass sat back down. "You think I can do anything about it?"

"No," Ryan said. "I just wanted to tell you."

"Well, you told me. Now your conscience is clear, if that's what was botherin' you."

"I guess you're right," Ryan said. He went back outside and picked up his gun.

It had taken him quite a while to learn to draw and shoot again. A stiff back, held rigid in a brace, and a virtually immobile left arm do funny things to a man's balance. Too, his recuperation had played tricks with his coordination, and he had trouble getting the Colt out of the holster with any kind of speed.

Once again he learned the value of patience. The long, slow days and nights, as well as his association with the Indian, who could sit for hours without stirring, taught him without words.

Because of his injuries, he would never be fast with a gun again. Before, he could draw and fire while most men would still be thinking about it, but that was impossible now. His only ally would be accuracy, and each day he practiced shooting until he had used up all the cartridges the old man had brought.

He would draw the pistol deliberately and begin firing. At first he thought that even his eyesight had been affected. He couldn't seem to hit even the largest targets. But he found that his eyes were fine, though the cut on his face was dangerously near the right one.

No, the problem was not his eyes. His hand was simply unsteady, and there was no way he could grip it with his left hand to make things any better. The pistol's kick jarred him, too, in a way he had never felt in the past.

It took considerable work and effort, but he got better. His hand steadied, and soon every cactus around the lean-to was riddled with holes, most of them placed exactly where he intended for them to be.

The old man went away again, and came back with more cartridges, along with dried beef jerky and even some flour. They had biscuits. Ryan even began to crave coffee.

There came a day when every shot went exactly where Ryan wanted it to go, or at least within an inch. His draw was still slow, but his aim was deadly. He wouldn't have to worry about protecting himself.

He could walk now, as well, walk without worrying about falling over, without having the old man beside him at every step. He was getting all of his strength back, though he knew he was gaunt and drawn.

He wondered how long he had been out there with the Indian. He knew that they had been through the seasons at least once. The winter had been bad, but the old man had brought blankets from somewhere, plenty of them, and they had survived the cold and even the one snow. The heat had been worse than the cold, but there was water somewhere nearby. Ryan didn't yet know where, but there was never a shortage of it when it was needed.

As his health improved, he thought vaguely about Tularosa, his sister, Kane, Virginia. Whatever he might have done was now irrelevant. Too much time had passed for him to make a difference there. Kane probably thought he was dead, and in this case Kane wasn't too far wrong. The difference in being dead and in being completely out of circulation was so small as not to be a difference at all.

In most ways, when he thought about it, Ryan never wanted to go back to Tularosa at all. It was as if everything had been burned out of him there in the desert. No love, no hate—nothing was left. It was only in talking with Virginia Burley and finding out how Kane had used her that Ryan discovered within himself the remnants of his ability to care.

McGee, along with Barson and Long, had special privileges at Kane's. They were the three men that Kane seemed to trust, and though he had a number of others working around the place, only those three had the run of the house. They even had sleeping quarters there, in an otherwise unused portion of the house, a long way from the rooms used by Kane and Billy.

They slept together in one large room containing three bunks and not much else. Barson and Long were there when McGee found them.

He told them about what he had seen in town.

Long's eyes glittered. "Maybe that Crabtree will do our job for us."

"What job's that?" McGee wanted to know.

"We talked to Kane this morning," Barson said. "He told us to get rid of Ryan tonight."

"We got something else on tonight," McGee said.

"Ryan comes first," Barson said. He smiled, showing the yellowed stubs of his teeth. "This time we won't let him get away."

McGee didn't much like Barson. He had slept in the same room with him for too long. The smell was bothering him, not that he would ever say anything about it. "Why didn't Mr. Kane say anything about this to me?"

"Maybe because you ain't seen him today," Long said. "What's the matter? Don't you believe us?"

"I believe you. I just thought . . ."

"Kane does the thinking. We just do what he says." Long ran his tongue over his dry lips.

"Sure. I know that." It seemed to McGee that Barson and Long were both taking too much of an interest in Ryan. For his part, he thought they might be making a mistake. Ryan had already proved a lot harder to get rid of than they had thought. "When do we go after him?"

"About midnight. At the shack. Then we'll go to get Billy out."

"Sure. Sounds fine," McGee said. He didn't mean it, though.

"Why don't you take a little siesta?" Barson said. "That's what me and Long are gonna do." He was sitting on his bunk, and now he put his feet up on it and leaned back.

"Good idea," McGee said, but he couldn't sleep at all.

One reason that Kane had let Billy stay in jail until the end of the week was the time of month. He was waiting for the dark of the moon. He wanted the darkest night he could get.

Kane himself was going to the shack for Ryan, but he could no longer ride. He was going in a wagon. He was too fat and awkward to get on a horse, and too much of a load. He would wait and reach the shack after the others, not wanting the squeaking of the wagon to give them away.

It was only with great difficulty that he was able to climb into the wagon. Long watched him with a secret contempt, and Barson had to hide a smile. Though he was a huge man, Barson could climb like a cat.

McGee didn't think anything. His missing finger was throbbing to beat the band. He was just hoping that he didn't get anything else shot off before the night was over.

When Kane finally got himself settled, he said, "This time we don't toy with him. We simply kill him. I do, of course, want you to hold him until I get there. I don't want to miss anything."

They couldn't see Kane's face in the darkness. The night had turned out even better than he had hoped for. Not only was there no moon, but from somewhere a breeze had sprung up, bringing with it the smell of rain and a heavy covering of clouds. There was not even any starlight.

Kane clucked to the horses, and they moved off slowly, with a creaking of harness. The others rode on ahead. "Don't forget," he said. "Save him until I get there."

If anyone had asked, Kane might not have been able to explain why now he wanted to make sure that Ryan was really dead. In their last encounter, he had meant to hurt him, injure him severely even, but not necessarily to kill him. He had wanted Ryan to give in to him.

But things had changed. Part of it was that Kane felt almost certain that Ryan had come back at this particular time for a reason, and Kane did not like the fact that he had no idea what the reason was.

Could it be only a coincidence that the hanging and Ryan's return had coincided? Kane didn't think so, and as he rode along in the wagon, savoring the rare smell of moisture in the air, he thought about how Ryan might interfere with his plans.

About the ranch, there was nothing Ryan could do. That had all been settled long ago, legally and officially. Ryan's sister had been left the shack and an acre or so, but that was all. And that was all that Ryan would be able to get, even if he stayed.

He wouldn't be staying, however, and Kane would have to make sure of it. He could be a big problem later on. Not during the jailbreak. Kane hardly gave that any thought at all. It was afterward that bothered him.

One of the wheels of the wagon squealed on its axle, and Kane listened to it absently. Afterward, he thought. It was the one thing that really bothered him.

The problem was that everyone in Tularosa was going to know for a certainty exactly who had broken Billy Kane out of jail. There could be no real question about it.

Who was Billy Kane's friend?

No one.

Who would break him out?

Only his brother.

Everyone would be able to reason that much out, including the sheriff. Kane was counting on being able to hide Billy away, from the sheriff and from everyone else.

He was afraid he might not be able to hide him from Ryan, however. Ryan knew the country around Tularosa better than anyone, and he would especially know about The Mountain.

The Mountain had no real name, but everyone knew it. Kane, who had once been to Colorado, laughed every time he heard anyone call it more than a hill; but in the flatlands around Tularosa it was the closest thing to a mountain they had.

Although everyone had seen it and heard of it, very few had actually climbed on it or even gotten very close to it. It was a long way out of town, for one thing. For another, it was on Ryan's land—or what had once been Ryan's land. It was on Kane's land now.

Ryan had never been one to encourage visitors, and Kane was downright inhospitable, so there was hardly anyone who knew about the cave. Kane knew, having found it more or less by accident when touring his new acreage one day. He had never heard about it before. Not one of his men knew about it when he asked them, and they had been told to keep it a secret.

There was no doubt, though, that Ryan knew, and since the cave was the place where Kane intended to stash Billy, Ryan had to be put out of the way.

At least that's what Kane kept telling himself.

The first faint rumblings of the distant thunder woke Virginia Burley a little before midnight. Like Pat Congrady, she lived in a room right over her business. She had rented a room from another widow when she had first moved to Tularosa, but when her brother died, she took over his quarters above the cafe. It was convenient, and she didn't need anything better. There had been a time, a time with Ryan, when she had begun to think in terms of a house again, a house away from town and a life away from the daily cooking and cleaning and waitressing that she had to do, but she didn't think in those terms any longer.

She sat in her bed and listened. The thunder rumbled again, and she knew that the sound of it was what had awakened her. She also knew that she had been sleeping lightly and restlessly before the thunder ever began.

She got out of the bed and tried to straighten the twisted sheets.

Her cotton gown was damp with sweat. She would not be able to go back to sleep for a while.

She walked in the pitch darkness to a small table and found a match. She scratched it on the underside of the table, and there was a sharp spurt of flame. She lit the lamp that sat on the table, then went to sit in the wooden rocker near her bed.

It was Ryan's fault that she couldn't sleep.

She kicked her foot against the floor and set the rocker in motion. After she had returned to town that night, leaving Ryan to whatever Kane and his men had in mind for him, she had gone to bed and slept soundly. She had told herself that she had done the right thing, taken the necessary step to gain her independence, and that she shouldn't be troubled by it.

She hadn't been, not then. But later, when she saw what Kane was doing to Sally Ryan and when Ryan himself didn't return, she found herself dreading nightfall. She had spent more than one night in the rocker, watching the shadows that the wavering light of the lamp threw on the wall.

Gradually she had gotten over her restlessness and sleeplessness, though. For the last year, she had been sleeping quite soundly, or at least up until the time of Sally Ryan's murder. That event had cost her a few nights, but once again she had settled down and convinced herself that it was none of her doing and none of her business.

Now Ryan was back, and she was in the rocker. The way he looked—the scar on his face, the stiffness of his back, the way he held his arm in front of him—she shook her head. There was no way she could deny responsibility, though he had never accused her, never even mentioned the cause of what she could so plainly see must be the result of considerable physical suffering.

Of course that was the kind of man he was. He held no bitterness in him, never had, but he had possessed a sense of justice that at first she thought must now be missing.

It was still there, however. She had seen it in his face that morning, and she knew that he would do what he could about Billy Kane.

She wondered why she cared about Billy. After what his brother had done to her—mustn't think about that, she warned herself; mustn't think of the way this cafe came to be mine—why should she worry about what happened to Billy? She hardly even knew him. But she told herself that she knew enough about him to know that he wouldn't kill anyone, and that he shouldn't die for no reason at all. Unless being Kane's brother was reason enough.

Billy Kane wasn't the real problem, and she knew it. Neither was her sense of justice.

It was Ryan.

Seeing him again, talking to him, she realized that whatever she had felt for him in the first place was still there. Somehow she felt a great contempt for herself. Ryan would never have made her dependent on him. He would have allowed her whatever freedom she wanted. Why hadn't she realized that before?

She rocked and listened to the thunder, sounding hushed and far away.

It was too late to worry about her life with Ryan now. Whatever chance there had been had died that night at Shatter's Grove.


Kane snapped the reins and the horses picked up their pace. He didn't know how far behind he had gotten, and he wanted to get to Ryan's shack. He was afraid that his men might not be able to restrain themselves once they got their hands on Ryan. It would be a shame not to get there in time.

Almost as soon as he turned off on the road leading to the shack, he heard a horse coming in his direction. He stopped the wagon and waited.

The horse came to a halt only a few feet in front of him, but he couldn't see who was riding it. It was too dark.

"Who's there?" he said.

"McGee."

"What's the trouble, McGee? By God, you better not tell me that Ryan got away!"

"I don't know what to tell you, then," McGee said. He could

imagine Kane's face, red and twisted. He was just as glad he couldn't see it.

"What happened, goddammit? Who let him escape?"

"Nobody," McGee said.

"Nobody?" The anger in Kane's voice gave way to puzzlement.

"Nobody," McGee repeated. "He wasn't there in the first place. No one's there. The place is empty."

# Chapter Ten

The streets of Tularosa were deserted. Faint flashes of lightning gave the only light. If anyone had heard about the possibility of an escape by Billy Kane, no one seemed to care. Everyone who could get inside had already gone in; the visitors to town who had no place to stay had set up tents or were sleeping under their wagons. There was no one out and about, not even a stray dog.

No one, that is, except for Ryan, who sat on his horse watching the jail, which looked like a solid block of darkness distinguishable from its surroundings only by the light in its window. The light outlined the windows in neat squares, but it was faint and dim. Ryan supposed that Bass had lit only one lamp.

Ryan had been watching the jail since nightfall, concealing himself behind the dilapidated walls of what had once been Tularosa's only bathhouse. The owner had long since gone broke and departed, leaving behind his building, which soon fell into disrepair. It was the closest building to the jail, and on the opposite side of the street, so it gave Ryan a good vantage point. It was so dark that he knew no one could see him, and his only worry was that he might not be able to see Kane and his men when and if they did indeed attack the jail.

He had still not made up his mind about what to do, even though he was there. If he stopped Kane, the hanging would go on as scheduled, and Billy would die. It seemed that his only other choice would be to assure Billy's escape, but that might involve harming Bass or his deputies.

Life had been much simpler for the past three years than it was now, and Ryan momentarily regretted ever returning to Tularosa. Things had been much simpler when he was with the old man. There was nothing to life except sleeping and healing, a slow, inexorable rhythm, so that one hardly even noticed the passage of time.

That stage of his life had ended early one night when the *curandero* had awakened him by gently nudging his shoulder. It was clear to Ryan almost instantly that the old man was leaving. By now they understood one another fairly well, even without words.

The old man put his hands on Ryan's shoulders and spoke quietly to him for almost a minute. Ryan didn't understand much of it, but he understood the last word. *Adiós.*

The old man smiled in the darkness, and Ryan smiled with him. He didn't know why the Indian had to go, but he understood that it was necessary.

The old man turned, and Ryan watched him walk away. There had been no moon that night, either, and the old man in his black clothing was soon absorbed into the darkness. He was walking very slowly when he disappeared.

After he was gone, Ryan felt a powerful sense of loss. He felt it more strongly than he had when he realized what must have happened to his land. The old man had been a true friend, even though they had never had a real talk, even though they knew nothing about each other.

But that wasn't true. They knew each other in a way that very few people did, with that special relationship between the healer and the healed. Without the Indian, Ryan would have died.

Because of him, he had lived, and he knew that the old man would not have left him had he not thought that it was time. Ryan could take care of himself now. His body had knit itself back together as well as it ever would.

He still wore the brace, and his left arm still hung pretty much immobile, but it was clear that neither his back nor his arm would ever improve much beyond the way they were now.

He began to do more walking, leaving his lean-to and covering the area in a circle around it, making the circle bigger each day. He used the pistol to get his food now, and he cooked it for himself. Even the rabbits didn't taste as good as when the old man had fixed them.

Finally he began to roam for miles in one direction or the other, in more or less a straight line. When he recognized the signs of a town in the area, he retreated to his lean-to, but after a week of considering it, he decided it was time.

He knew that he could lose himself in a town as well as he could lose himself anywhere, and that was what he did. He got a job working cattle, kept to himself, made no friends, had as little contact with others as possible. No one cared, as long as he did his job and kept out of trouble. It wasn't easy, working with one hand, but he managed to adjust. He might have gone on that way forever if he hadn't happened to see the article about Billy Kane in a newspaper that someone had brought to town and left lying around in a barbershop.

When he read the article, he knew that it was time to go home, and whatever regret he felt, sitting there at well past midnight watching the dark and silent jail, he knew would pass. His body had healed as much as possible, but it was his spirit that needed healing now. He thought that process had at last begun.

As he watched a faraway lightning flash, he hoped that he was right.


"That bastard Ryan could be anywhere around here," Barson said. He, Long, and McGee were riding ahead of Kane's wagon, circling the long way around to the jail. Though McGee was listening, Barson's remark was clearly addressed to Long.

"Don't worry," Long said. "We'll get him."

To McGee, they seemed overly concerned. Ryan had been in town for more than a day, and he had made no move to hurt them. He hadn't even tried to see them. It seemed to McGee that a man bent on revenge would do something right off, not wait around about it.

"Maybe he's not interested in us," McGee said. "Maybe he just came back because this is where he lives."

"Not anymore, he don't," Barson said. He rode his horse close to McGee, who could smell both the horse and the man. The horse smelled better. "He don't belong around here at all," Barson went on. "He's just trouble."

"If he don't bother us, he's not," McGee said. The less he had to do with Ryan, the better. He'd lost all the fingers he wanted to lose.

"Just his bein' around bothers us," Long said. "If Billy just shot him the first time like he ought to, we wouldn't be here right now."

"Billy'd still be in jail," McGee said. "And we'd still be breakin' him out."

"Maybe so," Barson said. "But we wouldn't be worryin' about that bastard Ryan and what he might do."

McGee didn't say anything, and the conversation stopped. They rode to within a mile of the jail and halted. The wagon caught up with them.

The thunder and lightning had moved closer. It was Kane's plan to wait until the small hours of the morning, when he thought Bass and the deputies would be asleep, or at least not very alert. He didn't like the idea of the storm. It might keep them awake. It would certainly make them nervous.

"We may as well go on in," Kane said. "The rain might work against us when it comes."

"What about Billy?" Long said. "He got any idea about what we're gonna do?"

"Not unless you told him," Kane said. "I haven't been allowed into the cells very often."

Neither had Long, or anyone else.

"You mean, we're just gonna blow up the jail and hope he gets away?" Barson said.

"That's about it," Kane said.

"What if we kill him?" Long wondered.

"We won't. And if we do, it's no more than will happen to him in the morning, anyway. Let's just hope that he has the presence of mind to take advantage of the situation we present him with. If he does, then things will be fine. If not, well . . ." Kane let his voice trail off. He didn't have too much faith in his younger brother's ability to do anything, much less to think fast in a crisis. But it was the best plan he had been able to devise. There was no way he was going to ride into town with his men, guns blazing. He maintained at least the facade of a respectable landowner, and he was going to do nothing to damage that facade. Whatever he did would be done in secrecy and under the cover of darkness. He wanted no one to see him or his men.

"Well, we'll do what we can, then," Long said. "I just hope you ain't thinkin' of puttin' the blame on us if this don't work out exactly right."

"I'm not," Kane said.

"Well then, let's do it," Barson said. He rode up beside the wagon and uncovered the dynamite. "I know what my job is."

"Long?" Kane said.

"I'm ready."

"McGee?"

"Yessir. I'm ready."

"Then do it," Kane said.

The plan was simple. Barson was going to dynamite the back wall of the jail. Whichever law officer was guarding the cell would be stunned by the explosion, or so Kane hoped. Billy might be stunned as well, probably would, but they would pull him out of the wreckage, toss him in the wagon, and be off with him before the other lawmen recovered from their initial shock. If anyone did happen to recover too soon and put up a fight, then he would simply be killed.

Kane hoped to avoid killing. It was going to be difficult enough to keep Billy in hiding and stay out of jail himself without adding in the death of a lawman, but he would kill if he had to. No Kane was going to hang for the death of a whore like the Ryan woman.

Barson removed the dynamite from the wooden box under its heavy tarpaulin cover in the wagonbed. "These things have got a short fuse," he said. "You boys just wait for me over here somewhere. I'll get back before they blow."

He rode off and was swallowed by the night. The others watched the black rectangle of the jail, with the flickering light in its windows.

Ryan was watching, too, but he had chosen the best cover and the place that provided him with a sight of most of the jail, not all of it. He could not see the back, and the night was so dark that he could not see Kane and the others where they waited.

As he watched, the wind picked up, getting cooler and stronger. He knew that they were in for a real summer storm, the kind that sometimes came to the edge of West Texas in the summertime, dumping inches of rain in only a few hours, swelling the few creeks out over their banks and turning the hard, dry dirt into thick mud. Such storms were rare, but Ryan had seen them before. The smell of rain was stronger than ever now, and the bay horse sniffed the air and snorted, shifting its weight around.

Barson wasn't worried about the rain. He had ridden as close to the jail as he dared and gotten off his horse, walking the remaining yards. He put the dynamite sticks at the base of the wall and lit the fuse.

He didn't wait to see if the guard had heard the scratching of the match. He took off toward his horse at a shambling run, not looking back, hurled himself awkwardly into the saddle, and spurred the horse up. It responded, scuffing hard chunks of dirt up with its shoes.

Barson was not quite back to Kane's wagon when the explosion came. It lit up the whole area, and Barson could see Long and

McGee silhouetted on their mounts against the black sky. The noise was louder than the loudest thunder.

No one needed orders after that. They all rode hard for the jail, Long and McGee passing Barson as he turned his horse around. Kane rumbled along behind in the wagon, but he would not get too close. The others pulled their handkerchiefs over their faces as they rode, not that they would fool anyone.

Ryan heard the explosion and saw the flare of light, and though he had not been expecting it, he put his horse in motion instantly. He had a pretty good idea of what had happened.

He reached the jail moments before Kane's men. It looked as if the entire back wall was gone, the sun-dried brick blown inward and outward and upward in all directions.

Two men were staggering around in the rubble. One of them looked like Meadows. The other one was probably Billy Kane.

As Ryan arrived, the door from the office was opened, and Ryan could see someone outlined in it by the lamplight. It was Bass, holding a shotgun.

Long was riding hard for the jail when he saw the dark figure of Ryan on horseback. He didn't know who it was, but he knew it was someone who didn't fit into their plans. He drew his pistol and opened fire.

It is very difficult to fire accurately from the back of a running horse. Long didn't come anywhere near Ryan with his shots, but one of them struck Meadows, who tumbled backward into the loose bricks that lined the cell area.

Bass loosed a shotgun blast in the direction of whoever was out there. Ryan felt the wind of the shot as it whooshed by.

Higby ran around the outside corner of the jail with another shotgun.

Barson and McGee both fired at him with their pistols, and he ducked back out of sight.

Bass blasted away with the other barrel, then slammed the door to reload.

Ryan had no choice except to hold his reins and leave his gun alone. A one-armed man is at a real disadvantage in a gunfight on horseback. Barson and the others were firing at him now, the muzzle flashes from their pistols lighting up the night.

Ryan had to make a quick decision before Bass or Higby came back with shotgun fire. He was caught between the opposing forces, and he had not yet even made up his own mind about what his position was. He had to do something, even if it was wrong.

He rode the bay up next to Billy Kane. "Hang on," he said.

Billy looked at him vaguely. He might have been deafened by the explosion.

"Hang on!" Ryan yelled.

Billy seemed to get the message. He reached up and gripped the back of Ryan's saddle.

Ryan switched the reins to his useless left hand so they wouldn't fall and helped Billy with his right.

Billy swung up behind him.

The horses were all milling around, everyone in confusion.

"It's Ryan!" Barson yelled. "Shoot him!"

"Don't hit Billy!" McGee shouted.

Bass threw open the door and fired off a round of shotgun pellets. One of them struck Ryan in the arm. He dug his heels into the horse's side, and they were off and running.

Ryan wasn't sure how much chance he had carrying double, and he wasn't even sure where he was going. It was something he'd have to work out later.

Lights were coming on all over town. People were rushing out of doors.

Ryan knew that there would be a posse formed almost at once. Not only that, but Kane would be after him even sooner. He urged the horse forward.

"I hope you're worth all this trouble, Billy," he said.

"What?" Billy yelled. His ears were still ringing, and he thought that everyone must be having the same difficulties in hearing that he was having. He still hadn't quite figured out what was going on.

He recognized Ryan now, though he hadn't at first, and he was pretty sure that he was involved in a jailbreak. He knew that there had been a lot of shooting, but he wasn't sure who had been shooting at whom. None of the buckshot had touched him.

There was a tremendous roll of thunder, followed immediately by a blazing lightning flash that lit up the entire sky and seemed to hang in the air for a full minute. Ryan risked a glance back over his shoulder.

He could see Barson, Long, and McGee pounding along after him. They weren't risking shots, however, thanks to the fact that Ryan's back was well protected by Billy.

They would catch him soon if he didn't do something. They were already gaining on him.

There was another lightning flash, and then the rain began to fall, the drops as big as five-dollar gold pieces and almost as hard. They stung Ryan's face under his hat. The drops were scattered at first; then suddenly it was as if the sky had opened and the water was pouring out in a solid wall.

The storm would hide him, even if it made riding more difficult. But for how long?

It was only then that Ryan realized he was heading in the direction of Shatter's Grove.

# Chapter Eleven

The storm got even worse.

Ryan was soaked through in seconds. The water was pouring out of the sky so fast that the dry ground couldn't soak it up fast enough; the bay was splashing through it already, as if wading a creek. The wind was so powerful that it seemed almost capable of pushing them backward.

The lightning continued to flash, but Ryan didn't look back again. He thought that if he could get to the grove, he could easily get away from the men who were following.

It was slow going, but finally they got there, the rain still flooding down around them. With the water cascading down from the brim of his hat, Ryan could barely see the dark forms of the trees.

He managed to indicate to Billy that he wanted him to get off the horse. Then Ryan slid off as well. He wanted to lead the horse in among the trees, knowing that it would be even darker and harder to see among them.

Ryan grabbed the reins, and Billy held to a stirrup. They could hear the rain smashing and rattling the leaves of the trees.

They were just about to enter the grove when with a tremendous crash a bolt of lightning struck an oak not twenty feet away from them.

The horse whinnied pitifully. The hair in her mane seemed to stand straight up. Ryan felt his own hair rising under his hat, and there was a peculiar tingling all over his skin.

The tree exploded with a loud C-R-R-A-A-A-C-K! that rivaled the sound of the dynamite used in the jail. There was a strange smell in the air, and the tree was burning, even in the streaming rain.

Ryan's hat lifted off his head and flew through the air. It had been jammed down so tight and so heavy from the rain that he knew the wind hadn't lifted it. He looked back just as one of Kane's men fired again.

Ryan didn't hear the shot that time, either. He led the horse on in among the trees, then walked around to Billy.

"Are you all right?" he yelled.

Billy, still dazed and not quite sure of what was happening, shook his head. "I guess so."

"Hang on to the horse, then," Ryan told him, handing him the reins. "I'll try to slow them down."

In truth, they weren't coming very fast. The wind, rain, and mud were slowing them very well already. The burning tree gave just enough light for Ryan to see them.

He drew his pistol and fired off two shots. He didn't hit anybody. Conditions were not exactly ideal for shooting. He wasn't even sure they knew he had fired.

He shot again.

One of the figures stiffened in the saddle and then slipped backward. He hit the ground with a splash, which Ryan couldn't hear.

The other two stopped. Ryan could see the flashes from their pistols, and a bullet thunked into the tree nearest him.

He fired back, then turned and motioned for Billy to follow him. They went deeper into the trees.

The rain was not as hard in there, the trees providing a minimal sort of shelter. Billy's mind spun as he tried to adjust to the situation.

He knew that he was with Ryan, but who was that after them? The law? But why would Ryan have engineered a jailbreak for him?

He thought about the explosion at the jail. He had been lying in his cot when things blew apart. He had been hurled across the cell, the cot landing on top of him and protecting him from the bricks that pelted down around him.

Then there had been a lot of shooting, men on horseback, and Ryan yelling at him. What the hell was going on?

Billy realized that he was very frightened. Even though he was not in the jail, facing the prospect of hanging, he was frightened.

Lying in his cot, he had been thinking about what it would be like the next day. There would be the crowd, all the faces watching him. His brother would be there, and everyone from the whole town.

He wondered how he would manage to get up the steps of the gallows. He was sure his knees wouldn't hold him up, yet it would be embarrassing to have someone support him.

He had decided he didn't care about the embarrassment. He was going to die, so why worry about dignity?

When he heard the thunder and saw the lightning from the tiny window of his cell, he had thought at first it might be good news for him. Maybe it would be raining so hard that they would call off the hanging. But he had never heard of anything like that happening, so he didn't count on it too much. Probably everyone would be there just the same, standing in the rain and getting drenched, but determined to see him hang.

It was appropriate, he thought. That was what it was. Appropriate. He wouldn't want to die on a sunny day so everyone could enjoy it and have a good time. At least they would be suffering just a little bit along with him. He almost had a tear in his eye, thinking about it.

He had felt sorry for himself before, but this was just about the worst he had ever felt. And that was when the walls exploded in on him.

Now here he was, hanging on to a horse in the middle of the worst flood he'd ever seen, wet and miserable as a drowned rat, and running from someone who was shooting at him.

And he was with Ryan, the man whose sister everybody thought he had killed. What if Ryan had brought him out here to punish him personally? Maybe torture him before he killed him, to get revenge?

Billy whimpered to himself, and in his cowardly way began to think about some way he could get the jump on Ryan, get him with his guard down.

He couldn't think of a thing, but at least he was out of the jail. He slogged on through the trees, mud sucking at his feet.

Kane arrived at the edge of the grove, furious. Raging.

McGee was down, shot in the shoulder this time. He didn't have any luck at all where Ryan was concerned. Or did he? He was still alive.

Barson and Long had dismounted to help McGee.

"What the hell is happening?" Kane ranted, his voice loud enough even to carry over the sound of the rushing water. "Who is that with Billy? Goddammit, is that Ryan?"

"It's Ryan, all right," Barson said, lifting McGee up.

McGee's shoulder throbbed like fire, but he couldn't help thinking that the rain was a blessing. Barson was getting his first bath in years.

"We've got to find him," Kane said more calmly. "He'll bring Billy back in the morning for the hanging. We won't be able to stop them then."

"Maybe *he* wants to kill him," Long said, his thoughts paralleling Billy's own. "That might be why he took him."

"Either way, we've got to find them. Put McGee in the wagon. I've got to get out of here. There'll be a posse along any time now, as soon as they can get one together. The rain has slowed them down some, but they'll be along."

They got McGee into the wagon, and he lay down. He didn't mind the water washing over his face. It felt cool and good. The throbbing in his shoulder was matched by the throbbing in his missing finger. That damn Ryan had done it to him again.

"Don't come back without Billy," Kane said. "And kill Ryan. This time, kill him dead."

He turned the wagon and headed away, leaving Long and Barson standing in the rain.

"I don't want to go in there after him," Long said. "He's got the advantage on us. He'll know we're coming." Long's cruelty came out only when he was sure that he was in a strong position.

"Well, I don't see that we got any choice in the matter," Barson said. "Not if we're gonna stay around here."

"One thing," Long said.

"What's that?"

"I say we don't make any distinction about who we're shootin' at."

"You mean even if we shoot Billy?"

"That's what I mean."

"Kane would have our hides."

"Not if we kill Ryan, too. Blame it on him. Say when we were gettin' close, he put a couple of rounds into Billy for spite. Who's gonna say it didn't happen that way?"

Barson's mind was as heavy as his body at times, but he got the idea. "Won't be anybody there but us," he said.

"Nobody but Ryan," Long said. "And he won't be tellin' anybody if we do our job right."

"Sure would make things easier," Barson said.

"We'll tie the horses out here. Make it easier in this dark and rain," Long said, satisfied that agreement had been reached.

"Good idea," Barson said.

They tied their reins at the edge of the grove, a good distance away from the burning tree, and went in after Ryan.

They weren't too worried about him.

They had caught him in there before.

Ryan's foot slipped in the mud. He lost his balance and started to go down, grabbing at the saddle to steady himself. It was the chance Billy had been waiting for. He swung his fist at Ryan's head, clubbing feebly at him.

Ryan was taken by surprise, and combined with his slippery footing Billy's right fist was enough to drive him off his feet. He went down heavily into the mud.

Billy, stunned by his own success, did not know exactly what to do. He had never escaped from anyone before.

He thought of going for Ryan's gun, but he had no desire to put himself in reach of Ryan's right hand. He thought of taking the horse, but realized that the animal would be more of a hindrance than a help.

Not knowing what else to do, he turned and ran back the way they had come, his boots slipping and sliding in the slick mud.

His mind was full of confused thoughts. He didn't know what he was running to, and he wasn't sure what he was running from. He wasn't even sure where he was. He knew only that he wanted to get away from Ryan and to stay away from the jail. The thought of going back to the jail and facing the gallows that had been built for him frightened him so badly that a sob ripped from his throat.

Wet tree branches lashed at his face, and he fell down twice, landing on his hands and knees. He tried to run, at the same time wiping his muddy hands on his pants.

Not watching carefully in the darkness, he ran into a tree. He howled in pain.

Long and Barson heard him. They weren't far away.

"What d'you think?" Barson said.

"Somebody's hurt," Long said. Thinking about it made him feel good.

"I mean, you think it's a trick?"

Long was surprised. Barson usually didn't come up with an idea like that. "Maybe," he said. "We'll be careful."

The rain was not falling as hard now, but it was still making enough noise to cover their movements. They headed in the direction of the cry.

Soon they saw a figure staggering in their direction through the trees, arms swinging to ward off the branches.

"That you, Billy?" Long said.

The figure stopped, its head swinging from one side to the other as if trying to see who had spoken.

"Billy?" Long said again. He already had his pistol out.

"Who's there?" Billy said.

"Me and Mack," Long said. "Just stay there. We'll get you." He nudged Barson with an elbow.

"All right," Barson said.

They both opened fire.

A bullet sang through the leaves by Billy's head. Another splatted into the mud at his feet.

Billy just stood there as if his feet had rooted in the mud.

They fired again.

This time one of them got closer. The bullet ripped through Billy's shirt and singed along his side.

"Y-E-E-E-O-W!" Billy howled. He turned and ran back toward Ryan.

Barson and Long went after him.

Ryan heard the shots, knew what they must mean. He was standing by his horse, debating with himself about whether to go back after Billy or leave him to whatever fate there was in the woods that night. He had done what he could, gotten Billy out of the jail unhurt and with none of the lawmen hurt except for one. And maybe that one wasn't dead.

He'd kept Billy away from Kane, too, mainly because he had decided he might be able to learn something from Billy, something that hadn't come out at the trial perhaps, something that might give Ryan an idea of who the real murderer of his sister might be.

But Billy was scared and treacherous. Helping him didn't seem worth the effort if he was going to try to escape at the first opportunity. He wouldn't tell Ryan anything if he didn't trust him.

Why not just let him go? Let Kane have him, or the law. What did it matter, anyway?

The shots changed Ryan's thinking, however.

Billy didn't have a gun, so whoever was shooting at him wasn't interested in seeing him hang. Either Kane or the law was going to finish things right now, and Ryan knew the law hadn't gotten there that fast. Billy's own people were after him now. Ryan hadn't thought even Kane would do something that bad. He would help Billy one more time.

He left the horse and started in the direction of the shots. He hadn't gone far when he heard someone crashing through the trees.

Ryan was in a small clearing, and he stepped aside to see who was coming.

Billy came flying through the brush and fell sprawling into the clearing, sliding for several feet on his stomach and face. He got up and began to wipe the mud from his eyes.

Ryan could hear his pursuers then. He stepped out beside Billy.

Barson and Long came racing into the opening, guns drawn. They tried to stop when they saw a second dark figure beside Billy, but they were going too fast, and the ground was too slick. Barson was leaning backward, his arms pinwheeling, trying to find a purchase with his boot heels. Long, on the other hand, was falling forward, bent almost double, flailing his arms to keep his balance.

Ryan could have shot one of them, but he hesitated. It wasn't in his nature to shoot a helpless man, even if the man was Martin Long. Even if Long or Barson either one would have shot him as casually as they would have shot a rattler.

Before Ryan could decide how to react, Long crashed into him. They went down in the mud together at just about the same moment that Barson ran headlong into Billy.

The four men found themselves grappling in the mud. All of them had dropped their guns, and they were hitting and clawing with their hands.

Ryan, with only one hand to use, was at a serious disadvantage, especially since Long was on top of him, but they were slick from the mud and Ryan was able to keep twisting his body, not allowing Long to get a good grip.

Long swung wildly at Ryan's face, getting in a glancing blow off Ryan's cheekbone. Then he got one hand into Ryan's hair—Ryan had no idea where his hat had gone—and began gouging at Ryan's eyes with the other hand.

Ryan slid his good right hand up between his and Long's chests. It was a job made easier by the slimy mud. He got his hand over Long's face and began to push upward with all his strength. He could feel Long's mouth opening and closing.

Long finally let go of Ryan's hair and started to pull Ryan's arm.

Ryan pushed upward, steadily.

Long grabbed the arm with both hands. At that instant Ryan heaved the trunk of his body upward and threw Long over his head. Long released his grip and hit the mud on his back.

Ryan felt around for his pistol and found it. At least he hoped it was his. There was not a chance he would shoot it now. The barrel might be filled with mud. He could, however, us it as a club.

Barson was sitting on Billy Kane's back, holding Billy's face down in the mud with both hands pressed against the back of Billy's skull.

Ryan walked over and hit Barson on the side of the head as hard as he could with the butt of his pistol.

Barson pitched sideways without a word.

Ryan pulled Billy's head up by the hair. Billy was choking and sputtering, spitting mud, but he was all right. Ryan got him to his feet, steadying him as they stood together.

Ryan turned his eyes from Billy to see Long charging them. He pulled back his right arm and waited. Just when Long arrived, Ryan drove his right fist, the fist holding the gun, into Long's face.

Ryan felt bone break and cartilage pop.

Long seemed almost to hang motionless for a second; then he fell like a plumb bob, making a loud splat in the mud.

Ryan looked around, trying to orient himself. It wasn't easy in the darkness. The rain had picked back up and was rattling through the trees with a sound like a Gatling gun.

Ryan took hold of Billy's arm and began pulling him through the trees. He stopped and picked up a sodden blob. His hat, he thought. He jammed it on his head, and watery mud ran down his face and neck.

He didn't bother to look back at Barson and Long. They wouldn't be following for a while.

# Chapter Twelve

It was just breaking day. Ryan hadn't slept much. He was too cold and too wet for sleep, though he was tired clear through and his back felt as if he had a hot poker for a backbone.

Billy, on the other hand, had slept ever since they had arrived at the cave and gotten in out of the storm. He was sprawled out in the dirt, snoring.

Ryan looked out at the sunrise. It was going to be another clear, hot day, and after a few hours of the blazing sun most of the ground would be as hard as before the rainfall. Most of the water had run off into the few creeks before the ground could soak it up, and Ryan wouldn't have been surprised to hear about flash floods in the country round about.

He wanted to get out of the cave as soon as he could. He didn't know whether there was anyone else who was familiar with it or not, but he had been gone too long to count on no one's having found it. It was on Kane's land now, but for all Ryan knew, Kane might be conducting guided tours of the place. It wasn't likely, but it was possible. It was more than possible that Kane himself had looked over The Mountain and found the cave there. Ryan knew that he couldn't stay.

He didn't know where he could go, however. Certainly the shack would not be safe. Both Kane and the law would be looking for him there.

He gave Sheriff Bass a minute's thought. It had been dark, very dark, at the jail. Ryan was sure no one had seen his face, so Bass would first suspect Kane. Unfortunately, all Kane had to do in this case was to tell the truth—that Ryan had Billy. Bass might even believe him, and if he did, Ryan would be caught in the middle.

There wasn't any question that Ryan was going to have to turn Billy back over to Bass sooner or later. Now that he had him, though, it seemed like a good idea to find out what, if anything, Billy really knew about Sally's murder. It might just be possible for Ryan to locate the real killer before he took Billy in.

Or it might turn out that the jury had been right and that Ryan's own feelings were wrong. Ryan didn't think so. There seemed to be too many others who felt the way he did.

He walked over and nudged Billy with the toe of his boot. Billy stirred but didn't wake up. Ryan nudged harder.

Billy turned over. His clothes were caked and wet. He blinked his eyes, then sat up suddenly. "Wh . . . wha . . .?"

He saw Ryan, and his head began to turn from side to side. His body jerked as if he wanted to get up and run but wasn't sure about how to do it.

"Don't worry about it," Ryan said. "You're out of jail, remember?"

Billy looked at him. He wasn't jerking now, but his eyes were wide. "What happened?"

"Your brother broke you out," Ryan said. "I stole you, which turned out to be pretty good for you. A couple of Kane's men were trying to kill you."

Billy looked guilty. Ryan hadn't mentioned that Billy had hit him and tried to get away, but Billy remembered.

"We left them back in Shatter's Grove," Ryan said. "I don't

think they were hurt too much. Might catch pneumonia, but then so might we."

Billy seemed to notice the condition of his clothes for the first time. He tried to brush some of the mud off, but it was too wet. It stuck to his fingers.

"It was quite a storm," Ryan said.

Billy stopped brushing. He didn't know what to do or say now. He was afraid that Ryan was going to do something to him, but he wasn't sure what. The events of the previous night were coming back to him more clearly. He could remember Barson throwing him into the mud and pressing his face into it. If Ryan had saved him, maybe he wouldn't kill him. But why had he saved him? Billy wanted to ask, but he didn't have the nerve.

Ryan saw the younger man's confusion. "I didn't bring you here to do anything to you, Billy. To tell the truth, I don't think you killed my sister. What I want to know is, who did?"

"I . . . don't know," Billy said. "I've been telling ever'body that all along. I just don't know. I went to see her, and she was dead. That's the truth of it, and that's all the truth."

The sun was fully up now, a dark red ball that in minutes would be yellow and hot as it came from behind the few hazy clouds.

"Why'd you go to see her, Billy?" Ryan said.

Billy looked down. "I liked her."

"I bet a lot of folks liked her, but they didn't go to see her."

"She liked me, too," Billy said. He looked back up and caught Ryan's eyes. It was the first show of spirit Ryan had seen in him. "I know you don't believe that. Nobody else did. But that's the truth, too."

"Your brother know you liked her?" Ryan said.

Something in Billy's face changed. "No. No, he didn't know about it. I never told him."

"Why not?"

Billy gave a bitter laugh. "You know why not."

Ryan nodded. "I guess I do." He paused. "You ever tell her about that night at Shatter's Grove?"

"I . . . I couldn't."

It was too bad, Ryan thought. At least Billy could have told Sally that Ryan was dead. Or as good as dead. That might have made things easier for her.

"I wanted to," Billy said. "I really wanted to. But you can see how I couldn't. I know she liked me, but she wouldn't have liked me if I'd told her that."

"She was supposed to marry Pat Congrady," Ryan said. "How much did she like you?"

"It was all over between her and Congrady. She told me."

Ryan didn't believe it. "She ever tell him?"

"I don't know. After you . . . left, she kept to herself for a while. Then, when my brother got the land, she didn't have much to do with anybody. I know Congrady talked it all over town that he was goin' to marry her, and lately he'd been sayin' it might not be long, but I never believed it."

"You didn't ask her?"

Billy shook his head. "I didn't want to," he said. What he meant was that he didn't have the nerve, but he couldn't say that.

"And he's the one who found you at the shack."

"He's the one, all right. Don't think I haven't thought about that part of it. Maybe he's the one that killed her, and just waited for me to show up so he could put the blame on a Kane."

Ryan stepped outside the cave. The bay was still tied to a scruffy stand of milkweed. He turned back to Billy.

"Why would he kill her?" He was thinking about the day before, about Crabtree stopping to talk to Congrady right after insulting Ryan.

"She used to talk to me about you," Billy said, avoiding the answer to Ryan's question. "She used to say how you'd come back someday. Lots of people in town, most of 'em probably thought you were dead. She never did, though. She said she had dreams about you."

Ryan thought suddenly of his own dreams of the caged eagle. "What kind of dreams?"

"She never said. I thought you were dead myself. I never saw how you could survive after . . . what we did."

Ryan thought about his arm and his back. About the scar so close to his eye. "I barely did," he said. Then he got back on track. "I was asking you about Pat Congrady. Why would he kill my sister?"

"Maybe he was jealous."

Ryan could tell by the sound of Billy's voice that even he didn't believe what he was saying. No one else in Tularosa would have believed him, either. Sally Ryan turn down Pat Congrady, a man with a solid job and a store of his own? Maybe a little tightfisted, but still a man who could be counted on to provide a home and be a good father to the children, they might have said, but not a bad man.

Not nearly as bad as Kane, no matter what his faults might be.

"Tell me something, Billy," Ryan said. "Just exactly how did my sister treat you?"

Billy looked off to the side, down at the cave floor, anywhere but at Ryan.

"Tell me, Billy."

"All right," he said. "All right. She treated me like a damn kid. Is that what you wanted me to say? Well, that's the way it was. Like I was some kind of stray that had wandered up and she had to take care of it. I guess she felt sorry for me." His shoulders slumped. "I guess that was it, sure enough. She felt sorry for me."

He looked up suddenly at Ryan. "Why would my brother break me out and then kill me?"

"I don't know the answer to that one," Ryan said. "Anyway, it wasn't him that was trying. It was Barson and Long."

"They knew," Billy said.

Ryan felt the sun warming his back through his shirt. The mud would be drying fast on their clothes now. "What did they know?" he said.

"They knew about me and Sally," Billy told him.

"How?"

"They followed me once. I don't know how they got onto me, but I saw them. I don't even think they knew I saw them, though." He clenched his fists at his side. "They treated me like she did, like a kid. They weren't even tryin' to hide, like they didn't care if I caught them at it or not."

"Why would they be following you?"

"I guess they just wondered where I was goin'. I had got to where I would visit Sally a lot. I wasn't around the place as much as I had been, and they didn't see me in town. They mentioned it once, but I didn't tell 'em anything."

"Would they have told Kane about it? About where you were going?"

Billy thought about it. "I don't know," he said finally. "They might have, or they might not. If he asked, they would. But if he didn't ask, they might keep it back. Keep it to themselves, so they could use it against me. They didn't like me very much."

Billy seemed to Ryan to think that everyone treated him badly, and he began to wonder just how deep Billy's own jealousy might have been.

"They might have killed her," Billy said.

"Barson and Long?" Ryan and Virginia had already thought of the same possibility, so he wasn't too surprised to hear Billy mention it.

"Yeah. They might have." Billy smashed his fists into his legs. "They would have done it if my brother told 'em to. If they did, I'll find out. And then I'll kill the both of 'em. You wait and see if I don't."

Listening to Billy's false bravado, it was easy for Ryan to see why so many others treated him like a kid. It was the way he talked and acted, which made it hard to treat him like anything else.

Billy broke in on Ryan's thoughts. "You ain't gonna take me back to the jail, are you? I didn't kill Sally. I swear I didn't. You can't take me back to the jail!"

"I won't," Ryan said. "Not for a while yet, anyway."

When Long got out of the grove, his mind was filled with thoughts of blue murder.

He had managed to get most of the blood and mud off his face, but he still couldn't breathe through his nose. There was no telling what kind of damage that goddamned Ryan had done to it. While Long enjoyed inflicting pain on others, he was not fond of his own hurt, and now his whole face was aching. There was an occasional sharp stabbing in the area of the nose, as well. He had put his hand to his nose, and it felt all soft and mushy, not to mention being about the size of his hat.

He had come to first. Barson was still lying there, snoring in the rain, just like he was at home asleep in his own bed with a nice fire going and good meal in his belly.

Long dragged himself over to Barson and slapped him in the face a time or two. Barson hardly moved.

Long got weakly to his feet and started kicking Barson in the ribs, not too hard at first, but harder and harder as he started getting a little of his strength back. It wasn't that he really thought the kicking would wake Barson up. It was just that he had to take his hate out on somebody, and Barson was the only one who was handy. Long was not a man to bear frustration easily, as almost any whore in Tularosa could have testified.

Barson came out of it and began to make snuffling sounds. Long stopped kicking him and kneeled down to slap him again.

"Wake up, damn you," Long said. He stopped slapping and got his hands under Barson's shoulders, hauling him upright.

Barson was shaking his head and trying to figure out what had happened, not an easy job when your skull is still ringing from being clobbered with a pistol butt.

"We got to get ourselves out of here," Long said. "Understand? We got to get back to Kane's place."

"Huh? What? Huh?" Even at the best of times Barson was not a brilliant talker. In his present addled state he was hardly coherent.

"Come on," Long said, pulling Barson to his feet.

Barson tried to stand, but it was as if his legs were made of feathers instead of bone. He sagged back down, and it was all

Long could do to hold him up. Long wasn't feeling too well himself.

"If we don't get out of here quick, the sheriff will have us for sure," Long said. "Can't you get that in your head?"

"Huh? Head? Huh?"

Long gave up on trying to explain. He hauled Barson back up and got the big man's arm around his shoulder. He started walking forward, with Barson's feet dragging through the mud.

Long managed a few steps before Barson's weight began to drag him down. He stopped to rest. He could see that it would take hours to get back to the horses at this rate. The cold rain washed over them, but it didn't seem to be doing much to revive Barson.

After taking a few more steps forward, Long stopped again. "You got to help, or I'm just going to leave you here. To hell with you!"

"Huh? To hell? Huh?"

Barson's mind didn't seem to be clearing noticeably. Long struggled forward for several yards.

It was about then that the thought of killing Ryan began to crowd out the thought of Barson's weight and everything else.

This was all Ryan's fault. His nose, the damned load of Barson that he was having to carry, the fact that the law might be on them any minute—all of it was Ryan's fault. Every bit of it.

Another ten yards and Long was even beginning to blame Ryan for the storm. If Ryan hadn't been at the jail, things would have gone fine. Long would be at home now, clean and dry. In fact, if they'd just killed Ryan the first time, none of this would have ever happened.

Well, Ryan was a dead man now. He and Barson had fouled up this time, but it wouldn't happen again. Not after Ryan had gotten them into a mess this bad. He was going to pay, and pay hard.

He began to think of the ways he would like to kill Ryan. Shooting him in the face or the heart would be too easy. He wanted Ryan to die a little bit at a time, so it had to be something slow.

A stomach shot was good. Long had seen a man shot in the stomach once. It had taken him nearly a whole day to die, and he had been in considerable pain, to judge from the way he took on about it.

Or maybe something with a knife. Long liked to use knives. A cut here, a cut there. Nothing too deep. Just enough to hurt and cause lots of blood. He'd heard the Indians could cut you a thousand times before you died. It would be fun to do that to Ryan.

Or broken bones. The thought warmed Long's savage heart. He could get him an axe handle and work Ryan over with it. Break his arms, his legs, his ribs. And then break open his head.

Thoughts like that got Long out of the trees and back to the horses. Barson was beginning to come around at last, and the rain had slowed to a mere drizzle. The stump of the lightning-struck tree still smoldered off to one side.

With a little pushing and shoving, Long got Barson into his saddle. The big man slumped forward, but he appeared able to hold the reins and stay on the horse.

"Think you can make it?" Long said.

"Huh? What? . . . Uh, yeah. Yeah."

It wasn't much of a response, but it was better than Long had been able to get before. What the hell, if he couldn't stay in the saddle, let him fall. Long had done all he was going to do. It was up to Barson now. If he made it back to Kane's, fine. If he fell off and got picked up by the law, well, that was fine, too.

Thinking of the law, Long looked all around. There was a little light in the sky now, but not much. The clouds were breaking up, and there were a few pinpoints of light above, though not enough to see by. There was no sight or sound of anyone nearby, or even in the distance. Long was sure they could make it all right. The posse must have decided the weather was too bad for pursuit.

"Let's go," he said.

"Go? Uh . . . where?" Barson still hadn't come all the way out of it, but he was sitting up a little straighter.

"Just stay close and follow me. Can you do that?" Long rode right over by Barson.

"Uh . . . yeah. I think . . . so." Barson shook his head as if to clear it, but from the expression on his face it was immediately obvious that he wished he hadn't shaken it at all. "Ooohhhhhhh," he moaned.

Long was getting angry with Barson now. Hell, here he was with a nose that was mashed all over his face and at the same time swelling up like a poisoned dog, and Barson was the one doing the complaining. It was almost enough to make Long want to reach out his leg and kick Barson off his horse and leave him right there. To hell with him.

Barson put his hand to the side of his head. There was a knot the size of a turkey egg on it, and it was very tender to the touch. The skin had been broken only slightly, but the pain was radiating out from the knot in waves.

"Ooohhhhhhh," Barson moaned again.

Long moved off. "You comin' or not?" he said.

Barson kneed his horse in the flanks and somehow managed to follow. Every step the horse took sent a new wave jolting through Barson's head.

If Barson had been able to think clearly—if he had been able to think at all—there was no doubt that his mind would have been running along the same lines as Long's, with both of them contemplating all the pleasant ways to bring about an end to Ryan.

The pain, however, drove any attempt at thought from Barson's head. It was all he could do to stay on the horse and keep up with Long, who cursed him all the way back to Kane's.

# Chapter Thirteen

Kane had gotten Johnny McGee back to the house and into bed. His wound was not serious, and the bullet had passed clean through. Kane poured some whiskey on it, listened to Johnny scream, and let it go at that. He figured McGee would be all right, and if he wasn't, too bad.

After that, Kane had gone into his office and had a drink from the same bottle of whiskey he had used on the wound. He hadn't used the whole bottle. That would have been wasteful.

He regretted taking the drink almost as soon as he did it. It was raw and burned the back of his throat. He should have put that bottle away and gotten out the good stuff, the stuff that was far too good to waste on the wound of a three-fingered gunman. He corked the bottle and put it away in a drawer.

He needed sleep, but he would wait for a report from Long and Barson. He hoped the report would be a good one. Ryan had caused him more than enough trouble the first time they had tangled. Where the devil had he been all those years, anyway?

Kane thought idly that maybe they *had* killed Ryan the first time. This new Ryan was probably just a ghost who had come back to haunt him and to punish him for the death of his sister.

Not being a man usually given to whimsical thoughts, Kane almost had to laugh at himself. But at the same time, he caught himself taking a nervous glance over his shoulder at the darkened corners of the room to see if there was anything lurking back there.

He forced his head around and looked down at the top of the desk where he was sitting. Ghosts! The thought was absurd. Kane wondered if he was getting old.

Finally he dozed in his chair.

A scraping sound in the room awakened him.

He sat up straight in the chair and opened his eyes. What he saw was not a ghost. It was Barson and Long, dripping and covered in mud. Long's face was almost unrecognizable, and Barson had a vague look in his eyes, as if they were focused on something no one else could see.

"My God," Kane said, looking at them. "What happened to you?"

Long had been thinking for several minutes about how to answer that question, which he was certain was inevitable. "Ryan happened to us," he said.

"Ryan?" Kane said. His voice was mild, but in the lamplight Long could see the color rising to Kane's face.

"He took us," Long said. He had thought of and rejected a couple of possible lies and decided to tell the truth.

"It wasn't my fault," he added. "Billy helped him." Part of the truth, anyway. Not all of it.

"Billy?" Kane's disbelief was plain.

"You think a one-armed man could whip both of us?" Long said. "Look at Barson. Billy pistol-whipped the hell out of him."

At the mention of pistol-whipping, Barson's fingers went to his head. Kane saw the throbbing knot.

"Why would Billy help Ryan?" The disbelief was gone, but the tone was colder than ice in January.

"I don't know," Long said. "You think he don't trust us?"

"Would he have a reason?"

"Not one that I can think of," Long said. His beady black eyes stared straight at Kane, though he wanted to cut them toward Barson to see if the big man was about to blurt out anything. He needn't have worried. Barson was still generally unaware of what was going on.

Kane didn't try to stare Long down. He knew that Long would win any such contest that they engaged in. Like a snake, Long never seemed to blink.

"What would Ryan be wanting with Billy?" Kane said.

"I don't know that, either," Long said. "Not unless he just wants to cheat the state and kill him himself."

"Or unless he thinks Billy knows something that didn't come out at the trial. Do you think that could be it?"

Again their eyes locked briefly. "Don't have any idea," Long said.

"He could have been saving Billy from us just to be sure he got hanged this morning," Kane said.

"That could be it, all right," Long said.

Barson said nothing during any of this. Now and then a low moan would escape him.

"Well," Kane said, "no matter what, we've got to find out. You've got time for a few hours' sleep. Get Barson to bed and take a short rest. I want you to go to town early in the morning and find out what's happening. See what people are saying. Try to find out what Sheriff Bass has on his mind. Then let me know."

Long didn't think much of his assignment, but Barson wasn't going to be up to it, and McGee had been shot. "How's McGee?" he said. It wasn't that he cared. He was just curious.

"He'll be all right," Kane said. "But he won't be up to going into town by morning. That's your job."

"I wasn't tryin' to get out of it," Long said. "What if I should find out that Ryan brought Billy back and they're goin' right ahead with the hangin'?"

"That better not happen without your getting back here to me and telling me," Kane said. His white face twisted in the lamplight. "If Ryan does try something like that, we'll have to stop it."

Thinking about McGee being wounded and Barson being addled, Long said, "How?"

"We'll worry about that when the time comes," Kane told him.

Ryan had no intention of going back to town, at least not until after dark. He thought they could risk part of the day in the cave, and then they would have to start moving around, avoiding both the sheriff's men and Kane's.

He spent most of the morning questioning Billy about what had happened the day of Sally's murder, but he found out nothing more than he already knew.

Billy had gone to the shack to see Sally. She was dead when he arrived.

Stricken with grief—and, Ryan surmised, a great deal of fear—Billy had lingered too long in the shack, not knowing where to go or what to do. He had been there when Congrady arrived.

"I tried to explain to him," Billy said. "But he wouldn't listen. He was like a crazy man, yelling at me about how I'd killed her and now he was gonna kill me. He nearly did, I guess. I think I hit him back a time or two, but nothin' like what he did to me. When he finished with me, he hauled me back to the jail and told the sheriff that I'd killed your sister."

"You know a man named Jack Crabtree?" Ryan said.

"He works at the stables," Billy said. "What's he got to do with this?"

"I'm not sure," Ryan said. "I wondered if he knew Congrady."

"I don't know about that. He knew Sally, though."

"I thought he was a married man," Ryan said.

"He is, I guess. If you call that married. He's fooled around some, if you know what I mean."

Ryan thought he knew.

"Anyway, that's not the way he was interested in Sally. I mean, he might have been, but I didn't know about it."

"What way was he interested, then?" Ryan said.

"Well, Crabtree might not care much about his wife, but he sure likes that old yeller dog of his. It got sick one time and wandered off. He like to have worn out ever'body in town askin' if they'd seen his dog and if they thought it could be dead or if they knew where it could have got off to."

Billy smiled, as if at a memory. "You know how Sally liked dogs?"

"Yeah," Ryan said.

"Turns out she was the one with Crabtree's dog. It had wandered clear out to her shack, sick as could be, weak and straggly, runnin' at both ends. Sally found it and nursed it, gave it some kind of medicine she made up. It got well, and she took it into town and gave it back to Jack. You never saw anybody so happy over such a sorry dog as he was over that one."

It was still cool in the cave, but the air outside was sizzling. The mud had dried on Ryan's clothes and was beginning to crack and flake off. He was sitting on the ground, with his back against the cave wall. It wasn't comfortable, but it was better than standing all day.

"She always did like to take in strays," Ryan said. He wondered if Crabtree had gone to see her to thank her for what she'd done. He wondered if Crabtree had ever tried to develop the relationship.

"She sure did," Billy said. "She even liked me."

Tularosa was buzzing when Long got to town. He had changed clothes and made himself presentable, not wanting to look like he'd been wading around in the mud all night, but there was nothing he could do about his nose, which now hurt worse than ever. It looked worse, too.

George Maze was one of the first people he saw. "Damn, Long," George said. "What happened to you?"

"I ran into a door," Long said. The way he looked, Maze didn't question him. "What time's the hangin'?"

"You haven't heard?" Maze said.

"Heard what? I come to town for the hangin'."

"Hell," George said. "You're way behind. Somebody broke Billy Kane out of the jail last night."

Long was not much of an actor, but he tried to pretend surprise. "I'll be damned," he said. "Who was it?"

"Tell you the truth, I don't think they know yet. Sheriff tried to get up a posse last night, but nobody'd go out. Storm was too bad. So he and a few men are out this morning. They won't find much, though, I bet. That storm we had probably wiped out any trace of a track."

That was something Long hadn't even thought about, but he was grateful for the news.

Maze looked shrewdly at Long's nose. "Some folks are saying that your boss was behind things."

Long just looked at him.

"Of course, I wouldn't say a thing like that myself," Maze said. "Not me. But you know how folks in this town talk. Whoever it was that did it, they blew up the whole damn jail. Shot one of the deputies, too."

"Kill him?" Long said. He hoped they had. He didn't like the sheriff or any of his deputies, and maybe they could lay it off on Ryan.

"Naw, but he'll be laid up for a while. Broke his shoulder."

"Too bad," Long said.

Something in his tone made Maze glance at him sharply, but Long went on talking. "Anybody seen Ryan around here today?"

Maze thought about it. "I don't think so," he said.

"You wouldn't think he'd want to miss this hangin', would you?" Long said. "You'd think it'd be a big event for him."

"Come to think of it, you would," Maze said. "I wonder where he is."

"I wonder where he was last night," Long said. Then he walked off toward Wilson's Cafe before Maze could say anything.

Maze stood and watched him go.

All the talk in Wilson's that morning was about the escape of Billy Kane. Business was booming, and Virginia Burley was kept hopping from one table to the next, but the conversations were all the same.

Ryan's name was hardly ever mentioned. Most people were mentioning Kane's name pretty freely, however. There wasn't one that doubted he was responsible for the jailbreak.

When Long walked in, there was a sudden break in the buzz of talk. All heads turned to see him take a table.

Then the buzz picked up again, but most of it was barely above a whisper. None of it was audible to Long. Virginia Burley heard bits and pieces of it.

"Look at that nose."

"How you think he got that?"

"Reckon he got hit by a brick?"

"Somebody hit him, more likely."

"Who you think done it?"

Long sat at his table and let the talk run on, and soon it turned back to other topics—disappointment at missing the hanging, speculation about the jailbreak and Kane's part in it, various theories about where Billy Kane was hiding right at that moment. Everyone was careful to avoid any mention of Long.

Long sat there until almost ten o'clock. Then he went back to Kane's to tell his boss that no one really knew anything at all.

"All right, then," Kane said. "I want you to get Barson up and go and look for Ryan. And you'd better find him. When you do, kill him."

"What about Billy?"

"Bring him back here. I'll see about what to do with him."

"He might not want to come."

"Bring him anyway."

"All right. What if we can't find them?"

"Try very hard. Meanwhile, I'll be thinking about what to do with you if you don't."

Long wasn't afraid of Kane, but for a minute he wished he was McGee, who would get to stay behind and nurse his wound. "You got any ideas about where to look?" he said.

"A few," Kane told him.


Barson wasn't much help. Hell, thought Long, he wasn't any help at all. He could hardly stay in the saddle, and he seemed to be halfway between going to sleep and passing out.

As the day got hotter and hotter, the sun blazed down and seemed to burn a hole right through the top of Long's hat. It was like a big yellow bullet up there in the sky, shooting a hole in your head. Long knew that the sun was bothering Barson even more than it was bothering him, but he didn't make any allowances. They kept looking in all the places Kane had named for him to search.

The first one was the shack.

"Damn, Ryan'd have to be plain crazy to go back there," Long said. "That's the first place the sheriff and the posse are gonna look."

"And once they look there, they won't be going back," Kane said. His face seemed even whiter to Long than it ever had, probably because Kane had been sleeping in the chair for most of the night. It wasn't a restful kind of sleep. "Ryan might hide out in the grove all night and then go back to the shack after the posse searches there."

Long had to admit that was a possibility. Ryan was plenty smart, and it was the kind of thing he would think of. Long's mind didn't work like that. He wasn't subtle, any more than Barson was. But he could recognize the validity of Kane's idea. "I'll go by there," he said.

"You do that," Kane said. "And search all around it. There might be a convenient place nearby for him to hide."

The next place was the cave.

"I thought about that," Long said. "I don't even think the sheriff knows about that place."

"Probably not," Kane said. "But you can be sure that Ryan does."

"All right. Where else?"

"In town. At Wilson's Cafe. It may be that Ryan still has some sort of special relationship with Mrs. Burley."

The thought of Virginia Burley brought a feeling of tightness to Long's groin. He had often thought about her when he was hitting some whore; about her dark hair, and how it would look if it was down and swinging from side to side as he slapped her face; about her dark eyes and how the tears would run as he bruised and bloodied her lips.

"Long? Are you listening to me?" Kane was staring hard at him.

"Yeah. Just thinkin'."

"About what?" Kane wasn't paying Long to think.

"About Ryan," Long said. "Why didn't he bring Billy back to jail?"

"That's worried me, too," Kane said. "I think I've got it figured out, however. He's going to use Billy to get back at me. He thinks Billy killed his sister, so he will somehow try to strike at me through my brother. An appropriate action, no doubt, to Ryan's way of thinking."

Long didn't follow the argument, but he didn't care. It wasn't what he had been thinking about in the first place. "Anywhere else we ought to look?"

"Maybe something will come to you," Kane said.

Nothing had, though. They had looked at the shack, and there were tracks all around it. The posse had been there, no doubt of that, but there was no way to tell if Ryan had been there, too. Long wasn't much of a tracker in the first place, and he didn't know anything about Ryan's horse's tracks in the second.

One thing for certain, there was no one there now. Long had left Barson with the horses and sneaked up carefully and quietly on the cabin, pistol in his hand. He'd almost shot a horned toad that skittered across his path, but that was about the only thing he'd seen. There was no sign of Ryan or Billy, not around the shack or the well or anywhere else.

The cave was a different story. They'd been there, all right, but they weren't there now. It had to be them. Long couldn't track, but he could see that horses, or at least one horse, had been around since the rain. Who else could it have been?

"Damn," he said. "Wonder how much we missed 'em by?" He searched all around the area, but there was nothing, no other sign.

Barson tried to help, but he didn't accomplish much. His eyes looked funny to Long, who thought it might be a good idea to get him out of the sun for a while. Long didn't know much about head injuries, but it looked to him like Barson might have got his brain shaken up, what there was of it.

There was no use in getting Barson any crazier than he was, so they rested for an hour in the cave. It was cooler in there, though the place was hardly large enough to be much shelter. Barson leaned against one of the walls and dozed.

Long thought about searching Wilson's Cafe. He was looking forward to doing that.


Long and Barson went in through the front door. There was no one in sight. They walked through the dining room and into the kitchen. Barson's little nap seemed to have cleared his mind a little, and Long had told him again what they were doing. This time, Barson seemed to understand.

Virginia Burley was in the kitchen, along with two other women, the cook and the dishwasher, both of whom were Mexican. All three of them looked at the door as it swung open.

"We're really not serving right now," Virginia said. "If you want lunch, we might be able to fix you a cold plate, but there's really nothing prepared." If she was surprised to see Kane's men standing in her kitchen, she did nothing to show it.

The two Mexican women watched them with large liquid eyes

that gave away nothing. They were used to keeping their faces blank in Tularosa.

"We're not lookin' to eat, ma'am," Long said. The polite tone of his words hardly expressed what he was really feeling. Virginia Burley had been helping wash the noon dishes. Her sleeves were rolled up, and Long could see the whiteness of her arms, how smooth and strong they looked. Her hair was up, but coming loose, and he wondered how long it would take it to fall if he could slap her as he wanted to.

"Well," she said, "what do you want?"

"We—that is, Mr. Kane—was wonderin' had you seen Ryan today. He wants to talk to him."

Virginia's mouth hardened. She put her hands on her hips. "You can tell *Mr.* Kane that I have no more dealings with him. If he wants Ryan, let him find him without me this time."

"That mean you ain't seen him?" Long said.

"It means whatever you want it to mean. Now if you don't mind, I have work to do." She turned to the sink full of dishes.

Long looked at her straight back. "Fine with me," he said.

He and Barson left the room. Long wondered what Kane would do now.

# Chapter Fourteen

There were times now when Ryan actually missed the old man in black and the days they had spent together. They had shared a time of silence and healing, and Ryan had grown used to the quietness, with nothing but the sound of the wind for company—the sound of the wind and the old man's serene presence. Sometimes whole days would go by with neither of them saying a word, days that nevertheless seemed somehow filled with a kind of communication.

When the old man left, Ryan had thought at first it would be good to get back among people again, to hear them talking and laughing, to see them moving around purposefully, going about the daily business of their lives. But he had been wrong. It took him awhile to get used to the noise and the jabber, the scurrying around from place to place. He became a man who kept to himself, said little, bothered no one.

At one time or another, the thought that he might return to Tularosa would come to him, but there were many ways in which that life seemed to him to belong to someone else, some other man that he had known once, long ago.

Now that he had returned, he wondered why he had.

His sister was dead, but he felt no blame for that. Who was to say it would not have happened even if he had been there?

His land was gone, but that had been taken care of while he was still with the old man, hardly able to move, much less to do anything about Kane.

And yet something had stirred in him, something called to the surface by Virginia Burley, something that had made him interfere with Kane's plans for Billy.

Already he was regretting it. After they left the cave, Billy began to complain.

The weather was too hot. He didn't like riding double. He was afraid of what his brother might do to him if they were caught. He was afraid that the posse would catch up to them and lynch him on the spot. He was hungry. He was thirsty.

Late in the afternoon, they went to the shack. Ryan scouted around the area carefully before going to the well.

"They've been here," he said. "But there's no one around now. We can get a drink."

"It's about time," Billy said, his voice whining like a saw in cedar.

Ryan let him drink first, while he looked around at the tracks in the already hardening mud. He couldn't tell much about them, not even that there had been separate visitors after the posse had left.

He considered staying in the shack for the night, but he knew that it wasn't safe. He couldn't trust Billy to keep watch, and he couldn't trust him not to sneak away. Besides, there was something he wanted to do in town. He figured the last place anyone would look for Billy was in town.

Billy didn't like the idea. "You're playin' me for a kid," he said. "You just want to take me back there and turn me in. I won't go."

Ryan tried to appease him. "I could have turned you in anytime, Billy. You're the one who conked me on the head, remember? But I came after you and got you away from your brother's boys. You think you can trust them? It looked to me like they wanted you dead."

Billy could vividly remember Barson sitting on his back and forcing his head down into the mud. He could still smell the mud and feel it blocking his nostrils. He shook his head. "But I ain't goin' into town," he said.

"Yes, you are," Ryan said.

There was something in his look that Billy didn't like.

Ryan took a step forward.

"All right, I'll go," Billy said. "I think you're just gonna turn me in or get me killed, though."

"No," Ryan said, "I'm not. There's a place where I think you'll be safe until I can clear a few things up."

"Where's that?"

"You'll see when we get there," Ryan told him.

Kane's first tendency was to yell at Long and Barson, but even he could see that in Barson's case at least it would do no good at all. Barson looked as if he weren't entirely sure what he'd been doing all day.

"Get him to bed," he told Long. "And then get back in here."

Long did as he was ordered. McGee watched him covering Barson.

"What's wrong with him?" McGee said.

"Got hit in the head. Hard," Long said. "Ryan."

McGee's phantom finger hurt, but not as much as his shoulder. It seemed to him like Ryan was gradually wearing them down. He noticed Long's nose.

"He get you, too?" he said.

Long put a hand to his nose, but he didn't touch it. It was still pretty tender. "Yeah. He got me, too."

McGee didn't particularly like Long. He worked with him, but that was different; you didn't have to like a man to work with him. McGee knew that most of the things he did for Kane were on the shady side, and it didn't really bother him much that they were. At the same time he recognized a difference between himself and Long. McGee was a little bit crooked. Long was purely vicious. He enjoyed what he did for Kane. And there were other things he enjoyed even more. McGee had heard about them.

"What are you gonna do about it?" he said.

Long's reptilian eyes glittered. "I don't know," he said. "Yet."

He went out of the room.

McGee lay back in the bed and watched him go. He was glad he'd been shot and wouldn't have to take part in whatever was being planned.

When Long returned to Kane's office, Kane was sitting at his desk. The afternoon sun was getting low, and the office was dim. Kane's pale face looked like the ghost of the full moon.

"You should have gone to the cave earlier," Kane said when Long was standing in front of the desk.

"You didn't say to do that," Long told him.

Kane steepled his fat fingers. "Perhaps not. It doesn't matter now." He pulled the tips of his fingers away from one another one at a time, then touched them again. "There's another thing that's bothering me," he said.

"What's that?" Long said. There was a note of suspicion in Kane's voice that he didn't like.

"You told me that Billy pistol-whipped Barson. I don't believe that."

Damn, Long thought. He had just told McGee the truth of the matter. Had Kane been listening? He wasn't afraid of Kane, but he didn't like to get caught in a lie.

"I think I know what happened," Kane said. "I think that Ryan took both of you, but you were too afraid to tell me the truth."

The truth was that Long had lied to give himself an excuse for shooting Billy, because shooting him would be easier than saving him. But since Kane was giving him an out, he decided to take it.

"I guess you're right," he said. He tried to look ashamed of himself, but he didn't do a very good job of it.

Kane didn't notice. He'd made up his mind, and he was satisfied with Long's admission. He knew Billy didn't have the guts to pistol-whip a housefly, let alone a man the size of Barson.

"It's all right," Kane said. "I think you must have gotten careless, and I can't see how a man in Ryan's condition, if it's anything like I've heard, could whip two men like you and Mack, but we'll let that pass. It's too late to do anything about it now. But we can't afford to let it happen again."

Kane stood up and walked out from behind the desk. Waddled was more like it, Long thought.

"I don't know what Ryan's doing here," Kane said. "I don't know what he wants with Billy, assuming he hasn't killed him already. And I am not a man who likes not knowing. Do you understand me?"

"Sure," Long said. He didn't understand at all, but he wasn't about to say so. Sooner or later Kane would get to the point.

"But I don't even care what he's doing," Kane went on. "I don't even care why he wants Billy. He is disrupting my life, whatever his plans are, and I want nothing more than to be rid of him."

Now Long understood. "How are we gonna do that?" he said. Nothing had worked out very well so far, and Long didn't see any way of changing things.

"There is one thing we haven't tried yet," Kane said. "I think you're going to like the idea."

Long listened as Kane explained his new plan.

Kane had been right.

Long liked it.

He liked it a lot.

Ryan waited until well after dark, until most of the people who had drifted into town to see the hanging had drifted out again and most of the citizens had long since gone to bed.

It meant that he had to endure Billy's whining and complaining that much longer, but he knew that he would not be safe even in the middle of the night. He couldn't chance going in any earlier.

When they got there, they rode as silently as they could through the back streets, the two or three blocks where there were actually houses, where people were trying to establish some kind of life for themselves. The houses were small, but several of them had fresh paint, and more than one was surrounded by a fence. There were flowers in some of the yards, though Ryan could hardly see them in the dark. He wouldn't have been able to identify them anyway. One or two of the more ambitious homeowners had even tried to establish a lawn, almost an impossibility in that country without hauling in water in the summertime.

All the houses were dark, their respectable owners asleep. Ryan wondered what kind of lives they must lead. He had difficulty even in trying to imagine what their days and nights must be like—storekeepers, bartenders, preachers, teachers—they all lived in a world that Ryan had never been a part of. He smiled, thinking about what they would make of his own life, of his fight in Shatter's Grove and his stay with the old man. They would understand him no more than he comprehended them.

When they reached Congrady's store, Ryan stopped.

"What're we doin' here?" Billy said.

"I want to talk to the owner," Ryan said. "While I'm doing it, you're going to wait here for me."

They were in the alley behind the store, and he thought Billy would be safe there. He wasn't sure, however, just how much Billy would want to stay.

"If anybody comes along," he said, "you can take off. I won't hold it against you. Or if you just get the urge to move along, take off. If I were you, though, I wouldn't let your brother's men get their hands on me."

"I'll wait," Billy said. He didn't sound too happy about it. "Who're you gonna talk to."

"Pat Congrady."

Ryan felt Billy give a little jump behind him.

"It's not you I'm going to be talking about," he said. "You don't have to worry about that."

He got awkwardly off the horse. It was even harder when there was someone else on with you.

When he was solidly on the ground, he said, "Believe me, Billy, I won't tell him you're here. What I'm going to say to him does have something to do with you, though."

"What's that?" Billy said. Ryan couldn't tell if he was worried or not, but he suspected that he hadn't quite gotten over his shock.

"I'll tell you when I get back," Ryan said. Maybe that would hold Billy there, he thought, as he moved off into the shadows.

He moved as quietly as he could up the stairs to the second floor room. One of the boards squeaked, but not loudly enough to wake anyone.

Ryan paused on the tiny landing at the top of the stairs. There was no light inside. He put his hand on the knob of the door and tried turning it slowly. There was no resistance, and he completed the turn. Then he pushed the door. It was not bolted, and it swung smoothly inward.

When he stepped inside the room, he could hear Congrady snoring lightly. He closed the door behind him and walked to the bed, trying not to trip over anything in the darkness.

The bed and Congrady's sleeping figure were merely blacker blobs in the dark room. Ryan reached out and prodded Congrady with his finger.

Congrady snorted and rolled over. Ryan prodded him again.

Congrady spluttered and sat up. "Wha . . . what?"

Ryan made his way to one of the chairs, mostly by feel. He sat down. "It's me, Congrady," he said. "Ryan. You ought to keep your door locked."

"I don't usually have . . . visitors, Ryan. Not at this hour. What on earth do you want."

"To talk a minute."

"Couldn't we talk in the morning?"

Ryan could hear Congrady shifting around in the bed. "Don't bother to get up. This won't take long."

"All right. What is it?"

"Jack Crabtree."

"What?" There was real puzzlement in Congrady's voice.

"You know him?"

"Of course I know him. I guess everybody in town knows him. What does he have to do with anything?"

"That's what I want to find out. He said some things to me the other day that I didn't like."

Congrady shifted in the bed again. "What does that have to do with me?"

"That's what I'm here to find out," Ryan said.

"I wish you'd say what you mean, then. You come in here in the middle of the night and start questioning me about Jack Crabtree, of all people, for no reason at all that I can see—"

"He stopped by to talk to you right after he said those things to me," Ryan said.

"Oh. Well, what did he say?"

"He said something about Sally. And he called me a liar."

"He ought to be more careful," Congrady said. "But I still don't see how that has anything to do with me."

"He was really eager to see Billy Kane die," Ryan said. "And I wondered why. I know he was fond of Sally, but I got to thinking—what if Sally really did like Billy Kane? And what if you found out about it? You wouldn't be wanting anybody to interfere with Billy's hanging, even if he really wasn't guilty and someone else was."

"And that someone else was me?" Congrady said, his voice tight with fury. "I'll tell you something, Ryan. If I wasn't afraid you might be holding a gun on me right now, I'd get out of this bed and kill you with my bare hands."

"Like someone did Sally."

"You bastard."

"I really wish people around here would quit calling me names," Ryan said. "One of these days I might have to do something about it."

"Let me tell you something, Ryan," Congrady said. "I'd love for you to try. But let me tell you something else first. I didn't kill your sister. Billy Kane did that, like I said."

"You were telling everyone you were going to marry her. That wasn't true."

"It was true. She would have seen that it was the right thing to do sooner or later. It was just taking longer than I expected. She would have come around."

Despite himself, Ryan found himself believing Congrady. "What about Crabtree?" he said.

"Hell, he's trying to get me to give him a job. Everybody in town knows about it. He says he's tired of workin' at the livery and smelling like a horse all the time. Ask around. You'll see."

"I will," Ryan said. "But why did he say those things to me?"

"I don't know. But everybody here knows how much he thought of your sister. He loved her as much as I did, except in a different way. She saved his dog for him, and for Jack that was enough. He would've killed Billy himself if he could."

Ryan was a man who liked to think he knew the truth when he heard it, and Congrady sounded like a man who was telling the truth. "I'm sorry I busted in on you like this," he said. "I had to find out, though."

"I guess you did," Congrady said. "I guess I don't blame you."

"Thanks," Ryan said. "I'll be leaving now."

He made his way to the door. He heard Congrady get out of the bed.

"I think I'll just lock that door," Congrady said.

# Chapter Fifteen

As he descended the steps, Ryan wondered what to make of his talk with Pat Congrady. If Congrady was telling the truth, and he seemed to be, then who had killed Sally?

Could it be that everyone was right and that Billy Kane was guilty? It didn't seem possible to Ryan. Billy was as convincing as Congrady, not that Ryan had ever really considered Congrady as a suspect in the first place. He didn't seem to be the type to kill, and he obviously hadn't put Jack Crabtree up to talking to Ryan. The story that Crabtree was just trying to get a job was too easy to check if everybody knew about it, as Congrady had said. Ryan didn't think Congrady would say something like that if it weren't true.

Ryan thought that he might have been avoiding one of the more obvious suspects simply because the thought was too unpleasant. It wasn't that Martin Long hadn't presented himself. Long had a reputation for being vicious, a reputation Ryan could certainly vouch for, and he was supposed to be especially rough with women.

And Long had known about Billy's meetings with Sally. Ryan could just imagine Long going to the shack and trying to get Sally to be nice to him in return for not telling Kane about his little brother's visits to Ryan's sister. Sally would not have suffered such insults lightly, and if she had showed any sign of fight, Long might have fought back. And he might have enjoyed it. He might even have enjoyed it too much. . . .

It was something Ryan would have to check out. Right now, though, he didn't know exactly how he could check it. Besides, he had to do something with Billy first.

"Billy? You still here?" he whispered when he got to the bottom of the steps.

"I'm here," Billy said. He was still sitting on the horse. "Nobody's been by here at all. This whole place is asleep. I think we could just stay here in the alley all night."

"It might be all right for that long," Ryan said, "but come morning it might be a little busier. I've got somewhere else in mind."

"Where's that?"

"I'll tell you when we get there." Ryan started leading the horse.

"Ain't you gonna get on?"

"It's not far." Ryan didn't say that he couldn't get in the saddle with Billy in the way.

"I'm gonna get in the saddle, then," Billy said. "I'm bustin' my butt back here."

"Good idea," Ryan said. He paced with the horse down the dark alleyway. Nothing was stirring. The only sound was the faint clopping of the horse's hooves and the creaking of the saddle.

"This is Wilson's Cafe," Billy said when they stopped again.

"That's right."

"We gonna have us a steak?" Billy laughed softly. He thought he'd made a good joke.

"This is where we'll be staying, I hope," Ryan said.

"Damn, Ryan," Billy said. "We can't stay here. Do you think

*139*

this woman cares anything about you? Don't you know . . ." He decided not to finish the sentence.

"I know," Ryan said. "That doesn't make any difference now. I have a feeling no one will look for us here."

"What if she won't let us stay? What if she tells someone where we are?" Billy was starting to whine again.

"If she won't let us stay, we'll go somewhere else. At least we should be able to get something to eat here."

Billy remembered suddenly that he hadn't eaten all day. "All right," he said. "It sounds like a good idea."

"I'll go up and wake her. You wait here," Ryan said.

"Don't be too long," Billy said.

Even in the darkness, he could feel Ryan's gaze on him.

"I didn't mean anything," he said.

"I hope not," Ryan told him. He moved away.

He was glad that Virginia lived above the cafe. Not many of the locals did, except for Congrady, but it was more convenient here than it would be among the houses, where someone was always looking out a window. Here they could stay on the second floor and be safe even if the sheriff was eating in the room below. No one would think to look for them here.

Or at least Ryan hoped no one would.

He climbed the outside stair and reached for the doorknob. The door was already slightly ajar, and Ryan's touch sent it swinging inward.

Ryan felt a sudden chill, as if someone had stuck the cold muzzle of a rifle against the back of his neck.

He stepped into the room, and his foot touched a pillow. He knew that something was very wrong.

The room was in a complete mess. Bedclothes were on the floor. Chairs were overturned. Something bad had happened here, and Ryan thought suddenly of Sally and how she had died.

Ryan made his way to the lamp table, mostly by feel. It was still upright, and there were matches in a glass holder. He struck one on his boot and lit the lamp.

The sight of the room confirmed what he had thought. There had been a struggle there of considerable proportions.

Then his eye was caught by a piece of paper stuck under the lamp base. On it there was a brief note written in pencil: "Ryan. I have the woman. You have my brother. Perhaps we could trade."

The note was not signed, which made no difference at all. Ryan knew who it was from. Kane had outfoxed him again.

Virginia Burley was determined not to show her fear. She was trussed up in the back of Kane's wagon, and Martin Long was sitting in front holding the reins. That was enough reason for any woman to be frightened, and she was no different from any other woman.

She was frightened.

She was also determined not to let Long know it.

She had awakened earlier to find him standing over her in her bedroom, with his hand over her mouth. She had tried to scream, but she could not even take a breath because of his hand.

"You just be quiet," he said. "We can have us a good time if you just be real quiet."

She wrenched her head to the side and tried to twist away from him, but he had been waiting for that. His hand tightened on her mouth and did not slip an inch.

He leaned closer to her. She could feel his breath hot on her face. "Don't move again," he said.

She paid no attention, shifting under the thin cover and trying to get a knee into his side.

He was too quick for her, moving away, still keeping his hand over her mouth.

"I told you not to move," he said. "But if you want to . . ."

He lay down on top of her. "Now move," he said. "Wiggle around all you want to. Come on!"

She lay absolutely still, hardly breathing.

After what seemed like hours, he got off and stood beside the bed once again. She could breathe a little through her nose, but his hand remained clamped over her mouth like an iron band.

"Now I want you to get up real slow," he said. "Real slow."

She put her legs over the side of the bed and sat up.

"Now," he said, "I want—"

She didn't listen to what he wanted. She threw herself backward on the bed and tumbled off the other side.

He was after her instantly, but she slid under the bed and out the other side before he could reach her.

She got almost to the door before his hand grabbed a hunk of her hair and jerked her backward, popping her neck in the process.

Pulling her by her hair, he whirled her around and slapped her backhanded across the face, then came back with the palm, the slaps sounding like gunshots in the room.

She felt the terrible sting as the blood rushed to her face, and her hair seemed ready to come out at the roots, but she continued to fight, kicking at Long's thin body and twisting this way and that. She flailed her arms in an attempt to strike him in the face.

The blows, when they struck, were so feeble as to have virtually no effect on Long. She could hear his laughter over the harsh and ragged sound of her own breathing.

Then her nails raked down the side of his face. She could feel the skin tear, and she felt the wet blood on her fingertips.

Long stopped laughing, but his grip on her hair tightened as he pulled her suddenly forward, wrapping his powerful arm around her body.

He was panting, and she felt his hot breath against her face. Then he pressed his lips against hers. His tongue worked between her lips, but she clamped her teeth together to stop its progress.

He pulled away and spoke, his face only inches from hers. "You like it. You know you do."

His hand tangled in her hair forced her head forward to his mouth again, and his arm forced her body against his. She was wearing a cotton gown, worn by many washings, and she could feel his hard body through it. He seemed to be giving off heat, like a wood stove in winter, but it did nothing to warm the coldness she felt inside, a coldness that reached into her very bones.

One of her hands brushed the pistol at his side. She managed to get her fingers around the handle and to begin slipping it from its holster. She tried to ignore the fatty feeling of his lips rubbing against her own.

He must have felt what she was doing. Suddenly he pushed her from him, hard, sending her reeling backward to strike the wall. She heard the thud of the pistol on the floor, and then she struck the door frame, her head hitting the wood with the dull sound of a mallet on a melon.

Long picked up his gun, kicked a chair out of his way, and walked over to where she lay slumped on the floor. She jumped up and butted him in the face.

Long screeched and fell backward, putting his hands to his nose. He had never felt any pain quite like the one he was feeling now, which seemed to start at his nose and shoot out all over his body, right down to his toes.

Virginia scrambled with her hand at the door, knowing that she had only a few seconds to escape. She found the knob, but Long was on her again.

Long dragged her down to the floor, his pain absorbed into a red haze that filled his head and blotted out the darkness in the room. He slapped her face, back and forth, back and forth. He straddled her body and got his hands on her throat. He clamped his hands together and began to squeeze.

Virginia screamed when he slapped her, but then her breath was suddenly cut off. Her neck was caught in an unbreakable grip and she found the thought of Billy Kane flashing into her mind—Billy Kane and the hang rope. She thought briefly and fleetingly of Sally Ryan.

And then she stopped thinking.


Long never knew exactly why he relaxed his grip before it was too late. Possibly it was because Kane had been so explicit in his instructions: "The woman won't be any use to us dead,

Long. I want you to understand that. We must have the quid pro quo.''

"Huh?" Long was not a stupid man, but he was ignorant. He had heard of a quid of tobacco, but he didn't know what that had to do with anything he and Kane had been discussing.

"Quid pro quo. That's Latin. It means that we must have an equal exchange. Something we can hand Ryan when he hands Billy over to us, as he must, of course, as soon as he sees that we have the woman.''

"I don't know about that," Long said. "We've used the woman against him before. She turned him over to us. He might not be in much of a mood to get her back. He might not even care about her this time.''

"You don't understand men like Ryan," Kane said. "He has what we call a sense of honor.''

"You think I don't?" Long said.

"I know that you do," Kane told him. "But not of the same kind. Your own sense of honor would lead you to defend yourself against insults, but it would not lead you to defend a woman who had betrayed you.''

"You're damn right it wouldn't.''

"And that is precisely where you are different from Ryan. While personal insults might not bother him, or at least might not move him to any action, a threat to someone he regards as helpless will no doubt cause him to come immediately and foolishly to the rescue.''

"He's dumber than I thought, then," Long said.

"Yes," Kane said. "And that is the difference between his sense of honor and yours.''

"I still don't think I follow you.''

"It doesn't matter. While we could possibly lure Ryan here if the woman were severely harmed, or dead, he most certainly would not be fool enough to give us Billy. Therefore, let me stress once again the fact that the woman must be delivered back here in good health. Do you understand?''

"I guess so," Long said, and he did. So that meant he couldn't keep on squeezing the neck of the woman he was now sitting on, as much as he would like to continue doing so.

He eased off on the pressure.

Virginia didn't move.

Long released his grip completely and put his face to her lips. He could feel the faint touch of her breath.

She was alive. He felt faintly disappointed, but then he hadn't really wanted to kill her. At least, he hadn't wanted to kill her so soon. He could think of a lot of things he'd like to do to her before he killed her.

Thinking about those things made him reluctant to get up, but he did. He fished the paper that Kane had given him out of his pocket and put it on the lamp table.

He had asked Kane about the note earlier. Long didn't like the idea.

"It's a risk; I admit it," Kane said. "I believe it's a small one, however."

"If the sheriff sees it . . ."

"Then I've made an error," Kane said. "But I think Ryan will go there, or send someone for her. If her loss is discovered by an employee, as it is likely to be if Ryan does not show up, then I suspect the employee will see that Ryan gets the note instead of the law. I want Ryan to *know* who he is up against."

"All right," Long said, but he had misgivings. There were too many "ifs" in it for him. He liked certainties.

Still, he had been told to leave the note, and he left it. Then he picked Virginia Burley up and tossed her over his shoulder like a sack of grain and carried her down the stairs. No one would be surprised if a man like Barson had performed such a feat, but Long's wiry strength was often surprising.

He put her in the wagon he had parked behind the cafe, taking only a few extra seconds to run his hands over the cotton gown and feel the contours underneath. The pain in his nose had subsided somewhat, and he was feeling an urge to be a bit more tender.

He also took a few seconds to tie her hands behind her back

with a piece of rope he had in the wagon. She had proved that she was not one to lie down and go along with being hauled off in the middle of the night.

They were almost at Kane's ranch house when she regained consciousness. At first she was disoriented by the motion of the wagon and the smell of the outdoors. Then the events prior to her blacking out came rushing back.

She knew that she was being carried somewhere, and she thought that she had a pretty good idea where. She also knew that her neck hurt from the pressure of Long's hands and that she had come near to dying.

Naturally she was afraid, but Long would never know it. That she was sure of.

And if they were headed for Kane's, as she was sure they must be, Kane would never know it, either.

She wouldn't let him use her again.

# Chapter Sixteen

Ryan's thought was almost the same as Virginia's. He was not going to let Kane use her against him again, especially now that he *knew* that Kane was using her, and how.

Still, he didn't feel that he could let Kane get away with taking her. Something plainly had to be done, but Ryan wasn't sure exactly what that something was.

He crumpled the note in his hand and shoved it in the pocket of his jeans. Maybe Billy would have a suggestion.

"You mean he wants to trade her for me?" Billy said when Ryan reached him. "What for?"

"I don't know," Ryan said. "What do you think we should do about it?"

Billy was stumped. No one had ever asked him for a suggestion before, and he didn't know how to respond. "What do you think he wants with me?" he said.

"I don't know that, either," Ryan told him. "Long and Barson didn't seem to be handing out party invitations, though."

Billy slipped down off the horse. "You're not gonna trade me, are you?"

"No," Ryan said. He climbed awkwardly into the saddle.

Billy sighed and relaxed slightly. He had been prepared to take off on the dead run if Ryan had said yes. The more he thought about Long and Barson, the more certain he was that he didn't want to go back to his brother. On the other hand, he didn't want to go back to jail, either.

He pulled himself up behind Ryan. His other choice seemed to be to stick with Ryan and see what happened. That wasn't a good choice, either, it seemed to Billy. He knew that Ryan at one time had felt a certain amount of affection for the woman, and he was fearful that Ryan might fight to get her back. Billy had already had more fighting in the last day or so than he ever wanted to have again. He thought about how his face had felt as Barson mashed it into the mud, how his nostrils and mouth had been clogged with the gooey stuff.

"Maybe we could steal her back," he said. "Like the jailbreak, only we'll take her from the house."

"It wouldn't work," Ryan said. "Your brother will be too much on his guard, and I want her back now. Not later. I don't know what might happen to her there." He didn't say that he was afraid of what might have happened already in the upstairs room.

"I don't see how you can get her," Billy said. "You can't just ride right in and—" He broke off. He had expected Ryan to be agreeing with him, or at least nodding his head. But Ryan wasn't agreeing. "You're not thinking about *that,* are you? There's no way we'd ever ride in there and get back out alive. They'd kill us, and her, too. I won't do it!"

Billy's voice was frantic, but Ryan ignored him. Kane's note had proposed a trade, but there could be no trade without a meeting. Who was to say what might happen at such a meeting?

"We've got to talk to Kane," he said.

"No, we don't. We don't have to do that. You don't know what he's like! He'll never let us out of there! I'm not going!"

"Yes, you are." Ryan's voice was cold. "If I say so, you are."

Billy didn't want to argue, but his fear of his brother was greater than his fear of Ryan. After all, Ryan had done nothing to harm him so far. "It's a trick," he said. "A trick. We'll ride out there, and he'll shoot us down as soon as we show our faces. I know he will."

"I don't think so," Ryan said.

"He will. He will."

"It's dark," Ryan said. "He won't see us coming."

"He'll have somebody watching for us. Long, or somebody. He won't let us just ride up on him."

Ryan thought about Long lying in wait for him. He thought about what he'd like to do to Long. He felt a warm glow spreading over his body, warming a coldness that had been in him for what seemed like years. It was like his blood had stopped flowing that night at Shatter's Grove and had only just now found the old familiar paths through his body.

He wondered for the first time if he had known all along, known without knowing, if that was possible, how Kane had taken him that night. Could he have somehow suspected that Virginia had helped Kane, that she not only had not sent the sheriff but had never intended to send him? Could that knowledge, which he must have had, even though he had never allowed himself to think it, really explain why he had stayed away from Tularosa for so long? Suddenly all the other things he had told himself seemed unconvincing, and it was as if he knew for the first time the real reason for his delayed homecoming.

And Kane was at the bottom of it. He had been kept away by Kane, or by Kane's schemes, just as surely as if Kane had killed him that night.

To tell the truth, Kane *had* killed him, or a part of him. Not his physical body, though he had surely done his part to kill that, but his mental body, if there was such a thing. Knowing that Virginia had betrayed him, even though he would never admit it, had caged his mind and spirit as surely as the eagle in the dream was held first by bars of wood and then by bars that he couldn't even see.

Now Kane was working on him again. And Long was in on it, too, and Barson and McGee. They were after him again, and they were using Virginia again.

Ryan felt his blood pounding in his ears.

This time they wouldn't get away with it.

Long dragged Virginia out of the wagon, took her inside the house, and threw her on an Indian rug in Kane's office. He threw her down somewhat harder than was strictly necessary.

Kane looked up. "I hope you haven't damaged our quid pro quo."

"She's alive," Long said.

Kane glanced at the woman. Then he got up from his desk and walked around to get a better look. "I warned you," he said to Long.

"Warned me, hell. She fought me like a damn squaw. She hit me in the nose. Hell, she hurt me worse'n I hurt her." Long's fingers went to his nose and touched it gently. There was a string of dried blood running from one nostril down past his mouth.

"You don't look much the worse for wear," Kane said. "She does."

Virginia's face was beginning to blacken in several places where Long had hit her. Her hair was in disarray, and one of her eyes was swelling shut.

"I hope he hasn't hurt you too badly," Kane said.

She didn't answer, but she looked up at him coldly.

"It will do you no good to be uncooperative, I assure you," Kane said. "You might at least speak to me. I told Long not to hurt you."

Still she remained silent.

"I should think you might be curious about why I had you brought here," Kane said.

"Whatever it is, I won't do it," she said. "I've done my last for you."

"And well rewarded you were for it, too," he said. "But never mind that. What I want from you now is relatively painless. In fact, you have no real part to play. I require only that you be here."

"Be here?"

"That is all. You see, your friend Ryan has something I want, but he seems reluctant to give it to me. I am offering to trade you for what he has of mine."

Virginia hated herself for asking, but her curiosity got the better of her. "What does he have?"

"My brother," Kane said.

Virginia realized that she had herself to blame for her situation, at least in part. She had helped convince Ryan that Billy Kane was innocent, and she had told him that there was something planned for the previous night. So some of the talk she had heard in the cafe was true. It was Ryan, not Kane, who had taken Billy.

"What makes you think he'll trade?" she said.

"Why shouldn't he? You and he were great friends at one time. I see no reason for that to have changed."

"I told him," she said. "About the last time."

"That is no reason at all," Kane said.

Long, for his part, wasn't so sure, but he had already had Kane's lecture about Ryan's sense of honor and didn't say anything.

"You see," Kane went on, "Ryan is not the kind of man to let something like that stand in his way or to keep him from doing the right thing."

Virginia thought Kane might be right, but she said, "He might not think I'm worth it."

"Worth has nothing to do with it. Sooner or later he'll be here. When he comes, we'll be able to do business with him."

"At least you could untie my hands."

"No, I don't think I will. You might prove to be a reluctant guest and try to leave. Other than that, however, we'll try to make you comfortable."

"Then keep him away from me," she said, looking at Long.

"He does seem to have been a bit rougher than I anticipated. But someone will have to watch you."

"Not me," Long said. "I need some sleep." He was tired, and he had no desire to tangle further with Virginia Burley, at least not that night.

"You can wake up McGee or Barson," Kane said. "Either one of them should be able to do the job."

Long left the room.

Kane helped Virginia to her feet. "There's a bed in the room next to this one. You can wait there." He took her elbow to guide her.

The room was small, with only the bed and a chair in it. There was no lamp, and the tiny window did not admit any light. She could see the dark sky through it.

"I won't be able to lie down," she said. "Not with my hands tied like this."

"No, I'm afraid not," Kane said. "But you can sit in the chair. It will be awkward, but it's the best I can offer."

He smiled at her. In the faint lamplight from the other room, he looked like a boar hog walking upright. She wondered if a hog could smile.

"Why do you hate Ryan?" she said.

He seemed surprised. "Hate? What makes you say that?"

"You have everything you wanted from him. You chased him away. You got his land. Now even his sister is dead. Yet you're still not satisfied."

Kane pushed her roughly to the wooden chair. She half fell against it, then righted herself and sat.

"Hate has nothing to do with it. He resisted me, and he was punished, though not enough. He should never have come back."

"But what about his sister? You're talking about punishment, and Billy should be punished for her death."

"Billy had nothing to do with her death. She was a whore."

Virginia was shocked by the blunt assertion. She had heard talk that Kane's men had started about Sally, but no one would have agreed with it.

"That's not true," she said.

"Nevertheless," Kane said, "Billy didn't kill her."

"I think you're right about that. I never believed that he did."

"What?"

"I said, I never—"

"I heard what you said. I thought the whole town believed that Billy was guilty."

Virginia decided to tell Kane what the town really thought. It could not hurt. "I don't think even the sheriff really believes that Billy killed Sally Ryan. Everyone wanted to believe it, though, because he was a Kane. It was your name and your actions that got him convicted."

Kane stared at her, apparently speechless.

Virginia was sitting on the edge of the chair, precariously balanced with her hands behind her. She tried to edge backward.

"After tonight," she said, "I'm almost convinced that you had Long kill Sally. He's certainly capable of it."

Kane seemed to smile then. "He would do it if I told him to, or perhaps even for his own pleasure. He enjoys hurting people."

Virginia believed that. She had firsthand knowledge.

"However," Kane went on, "I don't believe he killed the Ryan woman. If he had done it, I would have turned him in at once to save my brother."

"No one would have believed you if you turned him in. They would all have thought you were lying to get Billy out of jail. So you let Ryan get him out for you."

"Ryan interfered in my plans. But I'll get Billy back."

"And what then? Ryan will tell the sheriff where Billy is. If he doesn't, I will."

"We'll see. I don't think so."

Virginia knew then that Kane didn't intend to let her out of his house alive. Or Ryan either, if he came. She wondered again what drove the man, but she knew that he would never tell her. His comments about Ryan's having resisted him and interfered in his plans didn't quite ring true.

She sighed and slumped in the chair.

Kane watched her for a moment, then left.

McGee was waiting in the office. His shoulder was throbbing, but he felt all right. He had gotten one of the others to help him put a crude bandage on the shoulder, and rigged a sling for his arm.

"Long said you needed me in here," McGee said.

Kane thought McGee was a sorry sight. He was already missing a finger and now one of his arms was useless. And then there was Barson, who still wasn't really recovered from the blow on the head. Kane wondered why he was cursed with men like that.

"There's a woman in the next room," Kane said. "I want you to watch her and make sure she stays there."

McGee thought he could do that. He started for the door.

"And McGee," Kane called.

McGee looked back.

"Go get a pistol. You might need it."

McGee looked around the room, as if looking for someone who might be a threat to anyone. "What for?"

"Someone might come for the woman," Kane said. He resented having to explain everything to McGee and the others. Why did they have to be so stupid? It was bad enough that they kept getting hurt.

"Who?" McGee said.

"Ryan. Ryan might come for her."

McGee didn't like that. "What's he gonna do that for?" he said. He had just about had enough of Ryan. He was missing a finger already, and he was practically missing an arm. He didn't want any more dealings with Ryan.

"Never mind. Just get the pistol."

"I don't know if I can use it."

"You weren't shot in that arm. Now get it, or get out of here and don't come back."

McGee actually considered the options. He thought that if he just left and never came back, he might be better off. But where would he go? He didn't have many job prospects, and at least Kane took care of him. He went to get the pistol.

When he came back, Kane was at the desk, ignoring him.

McGee went right on by, into the other room. He saw Virginia Burley sitting on the chair.

"Miz Burley," he said, "I didn't know it was you in here."

"What difference does it make?" she said.

"None, I guess," he said. He walked over and sat on the narrow bed. "Now I can see why he thinks Ryan might be comin' for you, though."

"What will you do if he comes?" She looked at the pistol dangling in McGee's hand. "Shoot me?"

He laid the pistol on the bed and pushed it to the side. "I don't guess I would," he said. "Nobody said to do that."

"You'd do it if somebody said to?"

McGee thought about that, just as he'd thought about his choices earlier. "Yes," he finally said. "I guess I would."

# Chapter Seventeen

"She'll be in that room he calls the office," Billy said. "We could get her out of there."

They were sitting on the horse about a hundred yards from the house. There had been no one watching for them as far as they could tell, and Billy was trying to talk Ryan into an attempt to rescue Virginia without having to directly encounter Kane.

"There's a window into the office, and we could get in through there. That's where he'll have her," Billy said.

Ryan couldn't figure out why there was no one around, but it was probably because there was no good hiding place, he thought. There were a few scattered oaks, but not a one of them was big enough to hide a man behind, much less a horse.

Which meant that Kane would have the watchers in the house. He said as much to Billy.

"Maybe so. But maybe we could surprise them."

Ryan didn't think much of that idea. Kane would be alert and waiting, no matter what time it was. He started the horse forward.

"We ought to go around to the back," Billy said. "That's where the window is. It's a big one, right down to the ground. We could go right through it."

Ryan stopped by a tree. "I'm going to leave you here, Billy. You can wait for me, or you can leave. I just want you to know I'm not going to trade you for Virginia."

"They'll kill both of you," Billy said. He slid off the horse.

"I'll come back for you if I can," Ryan said.

Billy stood beside the tree and watched Ryan go. The house was a black lump in the distance, a light showing in only one window. Billy didn't know what his brother had in mind, but he was sure it didn't include Ryan's coming back for him. Nevertheless he decided to wait awhile. He didn't have any better ideas.

Ryan had no ideas at all, just the blood pounding in him again for the first time in so long he'd almost forgotten what it felt like. He thought that he probably should have taken Billy along and made the trade; after all, what was Billy to him? But he was wondering why Long and Barson had tried to kill Billy. Had Kane ordered it, or had they tried it to keep Billy quiet and to put an end to speculation over the death of Ryan's sister? If Congrady was innocent, and Billy was innocent, it could be that Long and Barson—and Ryan thought Long in particular—might have a reason for shutting Billy up and getting him out of the way. Ryan was familiar with Long's reputation, and the condition of Virginia's room tended to confirm that the reputation was well deserved.

Ryan hoped that Virginia was still alive. If she wasn't, then Long was going to be very sorry.

What Ryan wondered was how sorry he would be himself, and he thought that he might feel that he had lost something quite valuable, something that he had just found again after having lost it. He believed that his meeting with Virginia did matter to him, and that there was even a chance they could mean something to one another again.

If she was still alive.

There was no one waiting at the front of the house. Ryan wondered if they expected him to knock on the door. Knowing Kane, that was probably exactly what he did expect. He would be looking for Ryan to come in with his hat in his hand, begging Kane to take his brother back.

And what then? A simple trade?

Ryan doubted it. He suddenly thought that Billy might have a point, that Kane could never be trusted to do the right thing.

Ryan climbed off the horse and tied it to a hitching rail made of a rough cedar post. He started walking around the house.

His boot hit a stone and he almost stumbled. He stopped and stood quietly, but nothing stirred in the house.

He went on, his fingertips brushing the butt of his .45. He had cleaned it that morning at the cave, carefully getting the mud out of the barrel and cylinders, checking the action. He held his left arm stiffly across his body.

He came to the back corner and went around it. There was a pale yellow rectangle of light on the ground, cast by the lamp in the house. Ryan angled away from the wall, so that he would wind up past the rectangle and be standing in the darkness.

When he got to the point where he could see inside, he stopped. The window that Billy had mentioned was actually a kind of double door with glass panes in it. Ryan thought that it must have cost Kane a fortune, but he could afford it. Through the panes, he could see inside the room, but he could not see anyone.

He saw the corner of Kane's desk, and he thought that Kane might be sitting there, though he wasn't sure and had expected to see several men at least in the room.

He walked through the pale light up to the door and tapped on the glass with his pistol barrel.

Now he could see the whole desk, and Kane behind it, whiter than white in the lamplight.

Kane heard the tap and got up, moving to open the door. He moved slowly and awkwardly, as if he were moving underwater. Ryan thought that he had gotten even bigger in the years that had passed since their last meeting.

Kane pulled the door inward, and Ryan leveled the pistol at his huge stomach. "Hello, Kane," he said.

"I had hoped you might be a little more civilized about things," Kane told him. He sounded like a schoolteacher who'd had his feelings hurt by a favorite pupil.

"It's just that I remember you too well," Ryan said.

Kane turned his back as if he had no fear of Ryan's shooting him and walked back to the desk. He lowered himself heavily into the chair behind it and watched as Ryan walked over, gun in hand.

"You may as well put the pistol up," Kane said.

"Where's Virginia?" Ryan said, holding the gun steady.

"Somewhere safe," Kane said. "You didn't think I'd have her here, did you? You should know me better than that."

In the next room, out of sight, McGee held his own gun trained on Virginia Burley, ready to shoot if she made a sound. Her eyes were wide as she listened to the conversation.

"After all," Kane said, "you didn't bring my brother."

"I don't have him," Ryan said.

"But you found my note and just decided to drop in?"

"That's right. Now, where's Virginia?"

Kane was chagrined. He had hoped that Ryan would bring Billy with him, and he didn't believe for a minute that Ryan didn't have him or at least know where he was. "There was to be a trade," he said. "I thought that you were an honorable man."

"Only when I'm dealing with honorable men. Where is she?" Ryan's thumb cocked back the hammer of the .45.

"Shoot me, and you'll never know." Kane looked at Ryan appraisingly. "I must say you're a bit worse for wear since our last encounter."

"You and your men can take the credit for that. But it won't happen this time. This time, I'm ready for you."

"I doubt that," Kane said. "Why, you're no more than half a man. One shot and I'll have men in here who can take you down in a second."

"Probably. But I'm not going to argue about it. You won't be alive to see it." Ryan's finger tightened on the trigger. "Now, where—"

"I'm in here!" Virginia yelled.

Ryan glanced around, taken by surprise. He saw a flash of motion out of the corner of his eye, and then there was a gunshot. He started for the door of the other room.

Virginia had thrown herself out of her chair after yelling, and McGee's bullet had gone into the wall. She rolled across the floor, and his second shot went wide.

By that time, Ryan was in the room. Three years before, he would have made it much sooner.

McGee looked up at him and swung his pistol around. Pain shot from his phantom finger to his wounded shoulder, and he jerked the trigger, throwing lead into the door frame.

Ryan steadied his gun and shot McGee through the bridge of the nose, sending the back of his head up against the wall.

McGee pitched backward over the narrow bed, no longer worried about his missing finger or anything else.

Ryan looked back into the office, but Kane was gone. It was too late to do anything about him now. Instead, Ryan helped Virginia to her feet.

"Can you get these ropes off?" she said.

Ryan went back into the office and rummaged through the drawers of Kane's desk. He found a folding knife in one of them and returned to cut through the ropes.

"Can you use a pistol?" he said.

"I can in a minute, as soon as I can feel something again." Virginia shook her hands, trying to restore the circulation.

Ryan went over to McGee's body, shoving the bed aside. McGee's pistol was lying beside him, and Ryan retrieved it. He handed it to Virginia.

She handed it right back. "I can't hold it. My hands are stinging too much." She bit her lip, and tears sprang to her eyes as the blood started to flow into her hands freely again.

Ryan went to the door to keep watch, but no one came into the office. He wondered where they were. He was sure that Kane wasn't going to let him just walk out the double door and away.

He watched until Virginia joined him. This time she took the gun from his hand. "I'm ready now," she said.

There was still no one in the room.

"All right," Ryan said. "Let's go."


When Billy Kane heard the shots, the sound was greatly muffled by the thick walls of the house. He knew what it was, though.

Having no weapon himself, he didn't know whether to stay or go. Fear trickled through his veins and the top of his head started to sweat. The drops ran down his brow, and he wiped them away with his hand.

If Ryan was dead, they would come looking for him. But if he stayed very still and quiet, they wouldn't find him. Would they? Probably they would, and then Long and Barson would hurt him. They would hit him again and try to kill him. Thinking of the pain they could induce made him sweat even more.

The problem was, he didn't know where to go if he ran. They would just track him down and get him that way. He began to wish that he had never left the jail, that he had just stayed there and let himself be hanged. Then he wouldn't have to be afraid anymore.

Since he couldn't decide whether to run or stay, he chose the easiest thing.

He didn't move, not even an inch.


Ryan and Virginia crossed the room and slipped through the door. Ryan strained his eyes into the darkness, trying to see if anyone was outside waiting for them. Though it was beginning to get a lighter gray in the east, he still couldn't see well enough to recognize anything beyond rough shapes. If anyone was out there, he couldn't tell.

"They must be out there," he said.

"Who?" Virginia said.

"Kane and the others. He's not going to let us get away this easy."

"Maybe he's afraid."

Ryan smiled. "I don't think so. Not Kane."

"Well, we can't just stand here peering out."

Ryan looked at her. She was a fine figure of a woman in the cotton gown, and despite what Long had done to her face, she was still the prettiest woman he had ever seen. But what he liked best about her right now was the fact that she wasn't a bit spooked by what had happened. Some women, and plenty of men, too, would have wanted to sit around and whine about their injuries or about how it wouldn't be possible to escape so they might as well give up.

Not Virginia. She had a fierce look on her face and a pistol in her hand. She didn't appear to be a bit daunted by anything.

"All right," Ryan said. "Let's go."

They stepped outside into the darkness.

Kane had rousted Long easily. The snakelike man hardly ever slept more than halfway. It was as if the sound of a feather falling in the next room could wake him, and the shots from the other part of the house, though distant and deadened by several thick intervening walls, had brought him almost to wakefulness already.

Barson was another story. Whether because of his head injury or because he was naturally a heavier sleeper, it took both Long and Kane to get him to his feet and to a reasonable state of alertness.

"I thought you said Ryan was a 'man of honor,'" Long said. "Looks like to me he let you down." He gave Barson's shoulder a solid hit with his fist. "Wake up, you bastard," he said.

"I admit he disappointed me," Kane said. "I thought he would actually make a trade, one brother for one former sweetheart, even if she was a faithless one. I was wrong."

They dragged Barson upright. Long slapped him sharply.

Barson shook his head. "Wha'sa matter?" His eyes opened blearily.

"Get up," Kane said. "Ryan's here in the house."

"Who's 'ere?"

"Ryan," Long said, dragging Barson from the bed. "Get dressed, dammit."

Barson began to struggle into his boots, the only item of clothing except his hat he didn't sleep in. If anyone had asked him, he probably couldn't have told the last time he had taken off his pants or shirt. McGee wouldn't have to worry about the smell anymore, however.

"Ryan killed McGee," Kane said.

Long laughed. "A real honorable man," he said.

"I'm sure McGee shot first," Kane said. "Though I wasn't really watching."

Long laughed even louder. "As if that mattered to McGee."

"I'm ready," Barson said. He sounded almost awake. "Where's Ryan?"

"Probably halfway to Denver by now," Long said.

"Maybe not," Kane said. "He doesn't move very rapidly these days."

Long thought about the way Ryan looked. "I guess not. Well, are we going after them?"

"Yes," Kane said. "Come on."

The others followed him through the dark halls of the house back to the office. There was no one there.

"Check the other room," Kane said.

Long walked over and looked inside. "Just McGee," he said. "Lying on the floor."

"Never mind him," Kane said. "Let's go outside and look for Ryan."

Ryan couldn't move fast, but he was faster than Virginia, who had no shoes. There was a time when Ryan could have tossed her over his shoulder and carried her, but that was a few years in the past. He helped her along in the darkness, trying to locate the tree where he hoped Billy would be waiting.

They had gotten around to the front of the house, but Ryan couldn't quite recall where the tree was. He knew the approximate distance, but not the exact location, and he didn't want to risk calling out.

He touched Virginia on the elbow, and they stopped while he looked around, trying to get his bearings. There were only a few trees, and he could pick them out as the sky continued to lighten, but he could not be sure which one was the place where he had left Billy. And he could not see Billy.

He heard a sound behind them and turned to look. Long came around the corner of the house.

Ryan and Virginia started to hurry forward. Virginia stepped on a sharp stone and fell, a small cry escaping her lips.

Long heard her and fired twice in their direction.

The shots went wide, and Ryan knelt by Virginia. "I think I twisted my ankle," she said.

Ryan turned and started to fire at Long, but he saw that there were two others with him. By the sheer bulk of them, they had to be Barson and Kane.

"Give it up, Ryan," Kane called. "You might get one of us, but we'll kill the woman for sure."

"Don't listen to them," Virginia said. "Don't let them get you again because of me. I don't want that to happen again."

But Ryan knew there was nothing he could do. Kane was right.

"Let her go," he said. "I'll come over there. You can have me."

"Oh, no, Ryan," Kane said. "That won't work now. We're going to have both of you." He started forward. Long and Barson followed.

"Kill them!" Virginia said.

"I can't," Ryan said.

He lowered his pistol and stood waiting.

# Chapter Eighteen

Billy Kane watched from where he was crouching at the foot of the tree. He couldn't make out all that was happening, but he could see enough to know that Ryan and the woman had gotten away and then been caught. He had a sudden fantasy of himself stepping out from the deep shadow, confronting his brother, and demanding the freedom of Ryan and Virginia.

He knew, of course, that nothing like that would ever happen, but the thought of it gave him a moment of courage. Not enough courage to make him move even an inch, however.

He listened to what was being said.

"You killed one of my men, Ryan," Kane said. "I think you should be aware that a gallows is already built for a murderer."

"I don't think anyone would call it murder," Ryan said.

"Perhaps not. You can drop the gun now." Kane was close enough to see that Ryan still held the pistol loosely in his hand.

Long walked over and took the weapon before Ryan could drop it. He slipped it into his belt. Then he jerked Virginia to her feet. She fell against him, unable to put her weight on her foot.

"Get over here, Barson," Long said. "Hold her up."

Barson grabbed her arm roughly, keeping her upright.

"Now," Kane said, "where's my brother?"

Billy held his breath, waiting for Ryan's answer. The sight of Barson and Long so close to him had destroyed all the courage his fantasy had given him. His chest felt tight and hot.

"I don't know," Ryan said.

"Long," Kane said.

Long stepped to Ryan. He hit him in the left shoulder with the barrel of his pistol.

Ryan sank to his knees without a word. Whatever damage had been done to his back and arm had healed, but the pain had never completely gone away. The blow from the pistol felt as hard as a blow from a sledgehammer.

"Where is my brother?" Kane repeated.

Ryan didn't say anything.

Long hit him again, harder.

Ryan stretched backward, his back stiff, but he didn't fall over. As some of the pain eased, he regained his balance and came upright.

"Next time, he hits the woman," Kane said.

"What . . . do you want with Billy?" Ryan said.

Kane seemed puzzled. "He's my brother."

"He killed my sister."

"Hit him, Long."

Long hit him.

Ryan fell over on his side. It was a struggle for him to get back up. His left arm was totally useless.

"Stop it," Virginia said as she watched him. "I'll go with you. Just leave him alone."

"I'm afraid you are of no use to us now," Kane said. "It's my brother that we really want."

Ryan got to his knees again.

"Let me tell you something, Ryan," Kane said. "Your sister was a whore, but my brother didn't kill her. He never killed anyone."

"I didn't think so," Ryan managed to say. "You had Long do it."

Long hit him for the fourth time. "You lyin' bastard," he said.

"What's he talkin' about?" Barson said.

Ryan heard them as he lay there, the pain shooting through his body like liquid fire. He rolled onto his side. He was hurting more than he had on that night three years before. "You killed her, then," he said, his eyes lifted to Kane's.

Kane sighed, and his shoulders slumped slightly. "Yes," he said. "I killed her."

"I should have guessed," Ryan said.

"No reason way," Kane said. "The method was more Long's than mine, I have to admit."

Both Barson and Long were looking at Kane strangely. Virginia was horrified to hear him confessing so calmly to murder. She knew then for a certainty that he planned to kill her.

"I suppose you could say it was Long's fault, however, or Barson's," Kane said. "They're the ones who told me that Billy was seeing Sally Ryan."

"You killed her because of that?" Ryan said. He was trying to twist his body into a sitting position. No one was trying to stop him.

"It wasn't that, not entirely," Kane said. "Of course I thought Billy was stupid to go off seeing a girl that I couldn't stand and who was the sister of a man I'd come to hate, but the man was gone, dead I thought, and the girl was very attractive. Even I had to admit that."

"But you . . . killed her." Ryan managed to sit up, grunting with the effort.

"Yes, I did. I went to see her one evening after putting Billy to some chore around here to keep him out of the way. I got out the wagon and went alone. I told no one. It was easy to get to that place where she was living without going through the town. No one knew that I was there."

"But why kill her?"

"I had to. She refused to listen to me, and then . . . well, what happened is not important. Only the result."

"She wasn't a whore, but you said she was." Ryan was afraid that he knew now what had happened.

"She was!" Kane said. "But naturally she wouldn't admit it. Even when I offered her money, more money than she had seen for a while, I'm sure, she refused me!"

"And so you killed her." Ryan felt very tired, more tired than he had felt when the old man had found him on that day so long before.

"I . . . yes, I . . . killed her. I didn't mean to, but when she refused me and . . . said things, I hit her." Kane looked down at his hands. "After that, I couldn't stop. She would have told. People would have laughed at me. So I . . . killed her."

"And let your brother take the blame," Ryan said.

"That was his own fault. I thought of a number of things to keep him occupied for several days, but he got tired of waiting and went to see her without telling me. If he had only waited a few more hours, he might not have been found there and nothing would have happened. But the fact that it was his own fault doesn't mean I just let him take the blame."

"I don't know what else you could call it," Ryan said.

"I couldn't say that I did it," Kane said. "You can see that. I thought that he might get off at the trial. And when he didn't, I tried to save him from the jail."

"And Long and Barson tried to kill him."

"What? Tried to what?"

Long struck Ryan in the head, clubbing him to the ground. "Don't listen to him," he said. "He's tryin' to turn you against us. Let's kill him right now."

Kane appeared to be thinking. "Not here," he said. "Take them behind the house."

Barson dragged Virginia stumbling across the yard. Long slipped his hands under Ryan's shoulders and half carried, half dragged him after them. It was getting almost light enough to see as Kane followed them back to the house.

When they got to the back, Kane said, "Put them in the office."

"Why?" Long said. "It's time we got rid of them and went after Billy."

"Go where?" Kane said. "Ryan has to tell us."

"He don't look very likely to do that," Long said. "He's as tough as any man I ever saw."

"Nevertheless he'll tell us," Kane said.

Long was beginning to wonder about Kane. The fact that Kane had killed Sally Ryan had surprised Long as much as anyone, and while it didn't matter in the least to him, it made him wonder how much Kane could be trusted. Maybe Kane would try to kill him, too.

"What are you gonna do?" he said.

Kane told him.

When Ryan came to, he was sitting in a chair in Kane's office. They hadn't even bothered to tie him. He was too beaten, looked too helpless, to worry about.

On the other side of the room, in another chair, was Virginia Burley, still in her gown.

She saw Ryan looking at her. "Are you all right?" she said.

Ryan would have smiled at that, had he been able. He was far from all right, and it was almost funny that she would think he could be. He was no longer even sure that his left arm was connected to his body by anything except pain. "Where are they?" he said.

"They took that man out of the other room."

McGee, thought Ryan. He wondered what they had done with him.

"They took him out back," Virginia said. She glanced at the open door.

"Can you get up?" Ryan said.

"No." She struggled in the chair to show him that her arms were tied behind her to the chair back.

Ryan thought he might be able to get up, but he couldn't. He tried to move, but his legs didn't respond. It was as if the bones in them had been replaced with water. He might be able to lean forward, but if he did he would only fall on his face on the floor.

Kane loomed up in the doorway and came into the room. It was getting lighter outside, and Ryan could see Barson and Long behind him, but it was still dark in the room. The lamp cast flickering shadows on the walls.

"Now," Kane said. "We have disposed of the body of our unfortunate friend, Mr. McGee. He obviously didn't have much luck with you, Ryan. First his finger, then his shoulder, and finally his life. You killed him a little at a time, it seems."

Ryan said nothing. Kane and his men had killed more than a little of him, and he felt no sorrow at all for Johnny McGee, just a sense of regret that he hadn't been able to do something more to the rest of them. The sense of life and revenge that had at last awakened in him was still there, still driving him, but he was too weak to do anything about it. And besides, they still had Virginia. The situation seemed hopeless.

"You may as well tell us now, Ryan, where my brother is. As you can see, we have every advantage." Kane's fat face was smug in the lamplight, fat and smug and white.

Ryan could see their advantage, all right, but he wasn't going to tell them. Call it stubbornness or courage, he didn't care. He didn't care for himself, and he didn't care for Virginia. She had already shown her courage, and he knew that she felt the same as he did. Kane had beaten Ryan once, or almost beaten him, three years ago. He had beaten Virginia at the same time but in a different, more subtle way. It wasn't going to happen again.

"I'm not going to tell you," Ryan said.

"If you don't, I'm going to give the woman to Long."

Ryan looked at Virginia. Her face was a mask.

He looked at Long, who was grinning in anticipation, his fingers gently caressing his tender and sore nose.

"Then Barson can have her," Kane said.

Barson grunted with pleasure.

"What's the matter with you, Kane? Don't you want her? Or do you only use whores?" Ryan's mouth twisted as he spoke.

Kane walked over to his chair and drew back his hand, but he didn't strike. He lowered his hand slowly. "I won't hit you, Ryan. If I did you might not be conscious to watch what happens."

Ryan thought that Kane was probably right, but he felt a little of his strength returning. Not enough to do him much good, but a little. He still doubted that he could stand up.

Watching Virginia's face, Ryan said, "I'm not going to tell you."

Virginia showed no emotion at all.

"Very well, then," Kane said. "Long?"

Long stepped over to Virginia's chair and put his hand down the front of her gown. He squeezed one of her breasts.

Her face was stone.

Ryan looked away. He could hear Barson breathing.

"Watch, Ryan." Kane grabbed his hair and twisted his head around.

Long squeezed harder, and Virginia cried out in pain.

"Are you sure you don't want to tell, Ryan?" Kane said.

Ryan saw Virginia's lips form a single word: No.

"I'll tell," he said. It didn't matter to him anymore. Billy was innocent and Kane was guilty, but neither Ryan nor Virginia would ever live to tell the real story. Kane might very well kill his own brother to hide the truth, but what did Ryan care?

And then it occurred to him. Why kill Billy? Why not let the hangman do that job?

"Tell me, then," Kane said.

"Get Long away from her first," Ryan said.

Long reluctantly removed his hand and stepped back.

"Now," Kane said.

"One thing first," Ryan said.

"Nothing first. Tell me."

Long was already back beside Virginia.

"Not until you answer me. Why were Long and Barson trying to kill Billy?"

"That's the second time you've made that accusation," Kane said.

"And it still ain't true," Long said. "I don't know what the hell he's talkin' about. Do you, Mack?"

"Hell, no," Barson said.

"Do me one favor, then," Ryan said. "Ask Billy when you find him."

"Don't listen to that crap," Long said. "He's tryin' to get your mind off what we're doin' here."

Kane was suddenly furious. "If he's lying, why are you in such a hurry to shut him up? I think I had better listen to what he has to say. Go ahead, Ryan, tell me."

"There's not much to tell. Just ask Billy who was sitting on his back and trying to smother him in the mud."

"Can't you see he's tryin' to turn us against each other?" Long said. "You can't believe a word he's sayin'."

"Possibly not," Kane said. "You might be right. On the other hand, I see no reason not to ask Billy what he's talking about."

Ryan saw a flicker in Long's eyes, as if a shadow had passed behind them. Too bad for Billy, Ryan thought. Long will kill him for sure now. Probably Kane, too. The only one who will come out of all this alive will be Long, and possibly Barson. That was what revenge usually amounted to. It was never what you expected. For a second Ryan regretted ever having returned to Tularosa.

But then he looked at Virginia. If he hadn't returned, he might never have felt alive again, and even if it had been only for a few hours, it was worth it. He was sure it was worth it to Virginia, as well. She had told him something that she had no doubt wanted to say for years, and she would not have to live with the feeling of guilt any longer.

"I have your promise, then, that you'll ask Billy?" Ryan said.

"Of course," Kane said.

Ryan wondered what the promise might be worth. "And what about me and Mrs. Burley? You'll let us leave?"

"Naturally."

"All right, then. Billy's at the shack. Where Sally was living."

"That's a damn lie," Long said. "We searched there today."

"I know that," Ryan said. "So did the posse. We weren't there then. We went later. I knew it would be safe after it had been searched once."

"What do you think?" Kane said to Long.

"It might be the truth," Long said. "We could tell the posse had been there, like he said."

"And Billy is there now?"

"That's right."

"I believe you," Kane said.

"Good," Ryan said. "Just let us go now. We won't interfere anymore."

Kane laughed. "You certainly won't," he said. "Do whatever you want with the woman," he told Long. "Then kill them both."

# Chapter Nineteen

Ryan wasn't surprised to hear the words. They were what he had expected. Virginia's face remained impassive, and he knew that she, too, had not developed any false hopes.

If he was ever going to take action, now was the time. He pressed his feet against the floor to test the strength in his legs. He thought he might be able to move now.

Then the glass doors swung open. Billy Kane was standing there. He was holding McGee's pistol, which Virginia had dropped when she fell. It was pointed at Kane.

"Let them go," Billy said.

Everyone was surprised to see him, even Long. It took them all a moment to realize that he was holding a pistol.

Kane was the first to recover. "I'm glad you're home, Billy. Put down the pistol. You don't need it here."

"Yes, I do."

Long was slowly bringing up his own weapon. "Going to try to kill him again, Long?" Ryan said.

Kane swiveled his head to look. "Put it down, Long!" he said, his voice cracking.

Long lowered the weapon, but he continued to stare at Billy like a snake staring at a bird.

"They won't hurt you, Billy," Kane said. "You're my brother."

"Don't say that," Billy told him. "I don't want to hear that."

Kane looked hurt. "What? After all I've done . . ."

"I know what you've done."

Ryan realized that Billy must have heard Kane's confession, but he wondered if Billy had the nerve to shoot the pistol even so. Ryan could see that Billy's hand was shaking so slightly.

Something in Kane's face changed as he came to the same realization Ryan had reached. "You heard me, then?"

"I heard you. You . . . you killed Sally."

"It was an accident," Kane said. "She called me things, said things, and I simply . . ."

"You killed her. And now I'll kill you."

Billy clasped the pistol butt with both hands to steady them and pointed the barrel straight at Kane.

Ryan thought he could hardly miss, considering the size of the target, if he could only bring himself to shoot.

They all watched Billy, his finger tightening on the trigger, the sweat popping out on his brow.

Shoot, Billy, Ryan thought.

They never found out whether Billy would actually have done it.

"To hell with this," Long said. He raised his pistol and pulled the trigger.

There was a loud crash of the report, which seemed to echo from the walls of the room. Billy spun around and flung out the doors, hitting the dirt outside.

Kane rounded on Long, fury in his face and voice. "You shot Billy, you filthy—"

"To hell with you, too," Long said, and pulled the trigger again.

The bullet smacked into Kane's flesh with a dull thud.

Kane took a step backward, stunned, but apparently unhurt. "You'll regret this, Long," he said.

Long shot him again.

The bullet splatted into Kane's thick body. Ryan could see the red stains spreading on Kane's clothing, but Kane was still standing. He actually began walking toward Long, who was smiling thinly. Ryan got the impression that Long was enjoying himself almost as much as he would have had he gotten Virginia to toy with.

Long fired a third time.

Ryan could hear someone screaming, he thought, but his ears were ringing from the shots and he couldn't be sure. The smell of cordite filled the room. Ryan decided it was time to move, if he could.

He threw himself out of the chair toward Barson, who had been watching the events unfold with a stupefied look, unable to take any action, as if he were paralyzed by what was happening in front of him.

Ryan staggered into Barson, knocking the big man backward against the wall. Ryan pinned him there, pressing against him with his left shoulder, ignoring the searing pain that swept through him. With his right hand he groped for Barson's pistol.

His fingers closed around the pistol butt just as Barson's closed around his neck. Barson began to squeeze, exerting enormous pressure and almost immediately cutting off Ryan's breath.

Ryan could feel himself slipping into darkness, but he kept the pressure on Barson, not letting him away from the wall. He tried to concentrate on getting the pistol from the holster.

When he finally got it free, he raised it and pressed it between himself and Barson. His mind was blanking, and he wasn't sure just who had the muzzle pointed at his chest.

He pulled the trigger anyway.

There was a loud crash, and Ryan felt the fire singe him, burning him through his shirt.

But it was Barson who cried out and released his grip as he began to slide slowly down the wall, leaving a red streak at his back.

Ryan, gasping for breath, turned to the room.

Kane was on the floor, flopping like some gigantic catfish out of water.

Long was cutting the ropes that held Virginia, crouching behind her as she still sat in the chair.

Someone still seemed to be screaming, but Ryan could not make out who it was. The sound of the gunshots still rang in his ears.

Kane was trying to sit up. "Billy . . . Billy . . ." he said.

It was Billy who was screaming. Ryan realized it then. Billy was not dead, and he lay outside the door, screaming in pain.

Long jerked Virginia up out of the chair. "Don't try anything with me, Ryan," he said. "I'll kill her."

Considering what he'd already done, Ryan had no doubt at all that Long meant exactly what he said. The trouble was that Ryan also knew that Long was going to kill her anyway, eventually.

Long backed toward the door, keeping Virginia in front of him as a shield. "I'll be leaving now," he said. "After that, I don't give a damn what you do, Ryan."

Billy had stopped yelling, and Ryan could see that he was sitting up. He still had the gun. Long didn't appear to be paying him any attention. There was a large dark stain near the middle of Billy's chest.

Ryan thought that Billy was going to shoot Long, but then he saw that Billy's bleary gaze was elsewhere.

On his brother.

"Billy . . . Billy . . ." Kane said.

Billy steadied the pistol and pulled the trigger.

The bullet entered Kane's left eye and came out the back of his head, ending all the frustrations of Billy's life.

Billy fell over, already dead, but Long whirled on him and shot him once more to be sure.

Billy's corpse bounced up slightly and then settled on the ground.

Quick as a snake, Long had the gun pointed at Ryan again.

Somehow Ryan knew with an absolute certainty that Long was going to pull the trigger. He had only two choices: take the bullet or try to kill Long, at the risk of hitting Virginia.

Virginia's eyes told him all he needed to know. She would rather die than suffer whatever Long would do to her. It was worth the chance.

Ryan fired.

All the days of shooting after his recovery, all the practice, all the spent shells, had prepared him for this moment. He would never be fast, would never outdraw anyone. But he could shoot straight.

His only target was Long's head, and the bullet took off the top of it.

Bright drops of blood filled the air as Long jerked backward, his own pistol firing futilely into the air.

Long fell, pulling Virginia along with him. She struggled to free herself from his death grip as his boot heels kicked against the floor.

Ryan walked over, very slowly, but as fast as he could. He reached down and pulled on Long's arm, still wrapped around Virginia's waist. It was like a vise, but Ryan kept pulling until something gave.

Virginia scrambled up. Her gown was spotted with blood. "Is he . . .?"

"Dead," Ryan said.

"Good."

Ryan looked around him. Long lay at his feet, with Billy not far off. Back in Kane's office, Barson was apparently sitting against the wall, only the long blood streak giving away the fact of his death. Kane lay on the floor, his head shattered.

Of them all, thought Ryan, Billy was probably the least guilty, at least as far as Ryan was concerned.

There had been a time when he would have felt elation at the scene, Ryan knew, but that time was long past. There was a sense of rightness about it, though, almost a sense of justice.

Sally had been avenged by one who had loved her at least as much as her own brother, and Long and Barson had paid for all the things they had done in Kane's name and at his orders.

None of that changed anything.

Sally Ryan was still dead. Ryan's arm would always be useless to him and cause him pain. Virginia would never really forget the way she had given Ryan up to Kane.

But maybe Ryan would get his land back.

And one day Pat Congrady would find himself another woman to marry and forgive Ryan's accusations. He might even give Jack Crabtree a job.

Ryan would tell the true story of his sister's murder, and if there was a next time for something like that, perhaps the citizens of Tularosa would think twice before convicting a man on skimpy evidence and the fact that they hated his name.

"I think I have a horse out there somewhere," Ryan told Virginia. "Let's go on back to town."

"Yes," she said. She put her arm around Ryan's waist to steady herself. "Let's go back."

They turned away from the house and started in the direction of the tree where Ryan had left the horse.

This time he thought he could find it. The sun was up, and there was plenty of light.

# Chapter Twenty

That night Ryan slept alone in the place where his sister had died. Late, sometime after midnight, he had a dream, an old dream, one that he had dreamed before.

Through the haze of a shimmering heat wave he could see the trading post in the distance. He resisted the urge to spur up his horse; he knew that the horse didn't have much more to give. They both needed water and food, but water most of all.

The trading post was almost falling down when he got there. The logs and wood were rotten and seemed to lean crazily one way or the other. The hitching rail crumbled in his hands when he tried to tie the horse's reins to it.

He went inside, but there was no one there. He called out, but his voice echoed hollowly in the empty room. There were cans on the shelves, but they were covered with dust, as if no one had handled them for days. Dust from the ceiling sifted down on his hat.

He knew that there would be a well out back, however. There had to be, or there would be no trading post there in the first place. When he turned to go outside and look for it, he saw the eagle.

It was in a wooden cage about four feet long, three feet wide, and not much taller than the eagle himself. The bird would walk the length of the cage, turn, and walk back the other way.

Turn again.

Walk back.

Turn.

Walk.

The eagle's feathers on each side were worn away from brushing the sides of the cage in his walking and turning.

The dream changed slightly then.

Ryan grabbed up the cage, feeling a sense of urgency that he had never felt before. He rushed outside with it, stumbling over his own feet in his hurry.

He set the cage on the ground and ripped open the door, tearing the rotting leather thong.

The eagle paced toward the opening.

Without a pause, it stepped outside.

Its eyes looked longingly at the sky as the dusty wind ruffled its feathers.

Ryan hardly dared to breathe.

Then the eagle took a step into the wind.

It raised its wings, and flew, slowly at first, then faster, circling higher and higher in a widening spiral.

Ryan watched it until it was no larger than a speck in the sky, and then it turned and flew away.

Somehow in the dream Ryan was still with the eagle.

Or he was the eagle.

Far below him, a man was walking, a man dressed all in black.

The man looked up and saw the bird, and somehow the bird knew, Ryan knew, that a smile creased the man's aged face.

And as the eagle soared, the old man turned and continued walking . . . walking. . . .